"What sort of a man is he?"

"A gentleman," Lucinda replied. "Quite young—well, thirtyish, I suppose—and tall. Fred liked him."

"A fine recommendation," her mother said with a touch of acidity. "He must be a paragon if the cat likes him! Where does he come from? What is his family? Is he married? Really, Lucinda—"

"He is unmarried and has lived abroad for some years," Lucinda supplied hastily. "He wishes to settle down in the country and...and make something of a neglected estate."

"Abroad where? India, perhaps? He must have a fortune if he thinks to make anything of Pinnacles. Is the house in any fit state for entertaining?"

"We shall see tomorrow," Lucinda pointed out with a stir of excitement at the prospect....

THE COUNTRY GENTLEMAN
DINAH DEAN

Harlequin Books

TORONTO • NEW YORK • LONDON
AMSTERDAM • PARIS • SYDNEY • HAMBURG
STOCKHOLM • ATHENS • TOKYO • MILAN

This edition published April 1986
ISBN 0-373-31011-0
Originally published in 1985 by Mills & Boon Limited

For the Waltham Abbey Society of Change Ringers,
and their thirteen voices

CHAPTER ONE

THE FRONT DOOR bell of the Rectory jangled peremp-
torily, causing Cook to drop her wooden spoon into the
pan of boiling gooseberry jam and exclaim 'Drat!' Immediately afterwards, Mrs Calvert's little silver handbell
tinkled upstairs, followed by the more brassy tones of
the bell in the Rector's study. Annie, the maid, halted in
her precipitate advance towards the kitchen door and
dithered, not knowing which to answer first.

'Do you go to Mama,' said Lucinda Calvert decisively,
'and I'll answer the door. Father must wait his turn.'

As she hastened along the red-tiled passage from the
kitchen to the front door, Lucinda was thinking that her
life had been ruled by bells for as long as she could
remember, from the small domestic varieties to their
huge brothers in the church tower next door—Faith,
Hope and Charity, James and John, Raphael, Michael
and Gabriel—whose eight voices called the people of
Woodham to worship or work, told of sorrow or rejoic-
ing, and marked the passage of the hours.

She reached the door and opened it on a placid sunlit
scene. The townspeople were mostly at their work in the
fields, in their homes or shops, or at the powder-mill at
the edge of the town, but a few idlers stood about,
watching a company of soldiers from the near-by camp
marching along the road, their drill sergeant's hoarse
bellow informing them that Bonaparte and his frogs

would be hopping all over them before they'd learned to tell their left feet from their right if they didn't *shape*. A few pigeons strutted and cooed on the paving before the church door, the swifts darted and screamed about the eaves of the church roof, and a blackbird was calling nervously from the lilac bush in the front garden.

On the garden path a stout, glossy black cat with white boots and cravat and a tall, lean gentleman in beaver hat, elegant broadcloth coat, nankeen breeches and gleaming Hessians were contemplating one another with apparent interest, oblivious of the opened door.

'Yes?' Lucinda enquired.

Both cat and man started. The former recovered first, shot past Lucinda and disappeared down the passage. The man gave Lucinda a thoughtful glance which took in her auburn hair, last year's sprig muslin frock, the holland apron over it, and the smear of jam on her cheek, then removed his hat and bowed slightly.

'Miss Calvert, I collect? My name is John Harris. I trust that the flying feline is not trespassing?'

'That was Fred,' Lucinda replied. 'After the Duke of York. He lives here.'

'Yes.' Mr Harris seemed unsurprised. 'I thought he reminded me of someone . . . Is your father by any chance at home?'

'Is he expecting you?' Lucinda countered, for she tried as much as possible to protect her father from unexpected callers, who often seemed to think that a clergyman should be at everyone's beck and call.

'I doubt it, but I'd be most obliged if he would spare me two minutes.'

Mr Harris had an air of confidence which Lucinda found made him hard to refuse. She hesitated, catching her lower lip between her teeth in perplexity. The man looked respectable enough—indeed, he was better dressed than anyone she knew! He had cool grey eyes which were regarding her with some amusement, and she noted inconsequentially that his well-cut hair curled a little above his ears, and his mobile mouth seemed about to smile, without actually doing so.

'I'm but recently come to the district,' he said. 'To Pinnacles House, to be precise.'

'Oh, are you the new owner? We wondered . . . That is, it's stood empty for so long, and the estate so neglected. Pray, come in. I'm sure my father will see you.' Lucinda stood back to allow the visitor to enter the square hall, which was really a room of the old house. An inconvenient timber post rose from floor to ceiling a few feet within the door, and Mr Harris collided with it before Lucinda could warn him of its presence.

'Oh, I'm so sorry!' she exclaimed, but he seemed unperturbed by the incident, and remarked with interest that presumably this had once been part of the front of the house, with the upper floor jettied out.

'I think the whole house has been much altered about, and not always very sensibly,' Lucinda replied, disconcerted by the unfortunate start to his visit. 'I hope you're not hurt?'

'Indeed, no,' he replied, the incipient smile broadening on his lips.

Lucinda half-smiled in response, led the way to the door of her father's study, which was on the left of the hall, and scratched on it before entering, Mr Harris hard on her heels.

The Reverend Simon Calvert was not yet fifty, but he chose to behave as an elderly and mildly eccentric parson, and the effect was heightened by his extreme short-sightedness, which his steel-rimmed spectacles did little to remedy; as his study window was overshadowed by a large chestnut tree, the greenish gloom which pervaded the room did little to assist him in his visual difficulties.

'Ah!' he said, rising to his feet behind his desk as Lucinda and Mr Harris entered. 'You're earlier than I expected, and you've both come, which is a great help. Now, before we start, I must inform you that you must both be baptised members of the Church of England, and one or both must reside within this parish . . .'

'Father!' Lucinda broke in, but the Rector raised a commanding hand. 'Your father's consent will be necessary if you're not yet of age, but I shall come to that in due course. To continue—neither of you may have the partner of a previous marriage still living, except under very rare conditions, and you must not be within the prohibited degrees of relationship to one another. Do you know what those are?' He picked up a Prayer Book and seemed about to read out the relevant list contained in the back of it.

'Indeed, sir,' Mr Harris replied reassuringly, 'and I may say with confidence that I am unmarried, baptised, and resident within this parish, and so, I am sure, is your daughter. But I do not, at present, intend to marry her, nor, I believe, does she wish to marry me, so the question hardly arises! I am John Harris, the new owner of Pinnacles House.'

The Rector adjusted his spectacles, gazed severely at Mr Harris, and said in an injured tone, 'I thought you to be Will Plomer, but I see you are not. Really, Lucinda, what were you thinking of to let me make such an error? My apologies, sir! I'm delighted to make your acquaintance.' He extended a friendly hand, which was still holding the Prayer Book. Mr Harris removed the book with unobtrusive dexterity, shook the hand, and replaced the book in it.

'Ah, what is this?' The Rector peered at the book.

'Why, it's my Prayer Book! I'm much obliged to you, sir, for returning it. I can't imagine how I came to mislay it.'

Mr Harris kept a commendably straight face and made a vague reply, then continued, 'I thought I should make my number, as our naval friends would say, being but recently come to Woodham, and of a sociable inclination. I trust you will forgive the breach of custom, but I thought it might take some time for people to hear that I had arrived, and then find time to climb the hill to call on me.'

'My dear sir! Most sensible.' The Rector beamed upon him. 'Now, pray be seated.' He swept a number of books and papers from one of the smoking-chairs provided for visitors into an untidy jumble on the floor. 'Tell me about yourself.'

'Tea, Father?' Lucinda suggested quietly.

'By all means!' replied the Rector, vigorously ringing the bell on his desk. 'Sit down, Lucinda, and play hostess, if you please.'

Mr Harris, who had felt himself unable to take his seat while Lucinda was still standing, gestured an offer of the chair which the Rector had cleared for him, the other three or four in the room being encumbered with more books, but Lucinda smilingly declined and took her place by a small table over by the fireplace, first piling the books from her chair neatly on her father's desk.

The Rector embarked on a few words about the weather, which had been fine and sunny for a whole week, promising a good harvest if it could continue another two months, which seemed unlikely in England, and presently Annie came in with the tea-tray, having divined the purport of her master's bell by some means of perception known to good servants.

The cat Fred sidled in with her, unnoticed, with what appeared at first glance to be a piece of string hanging from his mouth, and sat down quietly under a chair until Annie had withdrawn, Lucinda had poured the tea, and the Rector had handed it and the crisp little biscuits which were Cook's greatest pride. Then he emerged from hiding, stalked ceremoniously across the room to Mr Harris, and laid an offering at his feet in the shape of a small, dead mouse.

The humans watched in silence, all three having caught sight of the cat as he emerged from the cover of the chair, and they stared at the offering with some surprise. Lucinda was the first to recover.

'Oh, Fred, how could you! Mr Harris, I must apologise. I am *mortified*!' She seized the fire-tongs from the hearth and went to remove the corpse, but Mr Harris, controlling his face with difficulty, took the tongs from her, picked up the mouse with them and inspected it carefully.

'A field or harvest mouse, I believe,' he said, with apparent interest.

'Most likely,' the Rector agreed, coming round his desk to look more closely at the specimen. 'We seldom have the domestic variety, as Frederick is an efficient hunter. Ah, yes,' moving his spectacles to and fro to focus better, his nose only inches from the body. 'Observe, dear sir, the small size and the length of the tail—quite as long as the body. The house mouse is larger, although also with a long tail, and the vole, which is also quite—er—popular with Frederick, is larger, thicker-bodied, and comparatively short-tailed.'

Mr Harris observed all these points with close attention, then looked down at Fred, who was sitting demurely before him, looking remarkably smug, and said, 'Much obliged to you, sir! A handsome gift,' and then appeared a little nonplussed, not being sure what he was supposed to do with the body. Lucinda went to his assistance, took tongs and corpse from him and carried them outside, closely followed by Fred, who had only lent the mouse and had a vested interest in its fate.

After putting both animals out in the garden and removing her apron, Lucinda returned to the study, replaced the tongs in the hearth, and settled herself to make polite conversation, hoping that it might not occur to her father to invite the visitor to luncheon, which was to be only cold cuts, with Cook so busy making jam.

'I've been for some years abroad in various places,' Mr Harris was saying, 'and thought it time that I should settle down. I've a fancy to be a country gentleman and try to make something of a run-down estate convenient to London. Pinnacles has, I understand, been un-occupied and neglected for some years?'

'Indeed,' replied the Rector. 'It was the seat of the Hook family for—oh, three or four hundred years, I suppose, but the line failed. Sir Robert Hook had no children by his first wife, and but one son by his second, the child of his old age. He died in 1798, having let the estate go down badly in his last years through poor health. The son, another Robert, had bought his colours and was more interested in his army career than in managing his inheritance. He perished in the Helder expedition, and there was no other family, so the estate has been on the market ever since.'

'Yes, I heard something of this when I proposed to purchase it. The land which marches with mine to the north also seems neglected. Is there another sad tale to tell of that?'

'Indeed, but of another sort. The owner lives at Horsing, some seven miles away on the far side of the Forest, and has no interest in the estate except for shooting. He has let the meadow and arable in the valley to the War Office for a military camp, and allowed the rest to run wild. We do not care for his sort, sir!'

'You find the presence of the military so close to the town a problem?' Mr Harris asked.

'Indeed, no! Our gallant fellows are well-behaved and kept under discipline, and their presence is good for trade. No, our objection is to the waste of good land and the throwing of labouring people out of their work,' the Rector replied, and Lucinda nodded silent agreement.

Mr Harris had appeared to be looking at the Rector, but he must have observed Lucinda's movement, for he turned his gaze on her, and met her eyes with a hard, calculating look which gave her a curious feeling inside which she did not much like, for it was disturbing and made her unaccountably uneasy.

The church clock reached the hour at that moment, and, after James and John had ting-tanged the four quarters, Gabriel's sonorous tones told the hour, effectively killing conversation while he did so, and causing Mr Harris to start and look about him in some bewilderment, as if he had mistaken the sound for the Crack of Doom. The Rector merely took out his pocket-watch and peered at its dial in mild disbelief before shaking it vigorously and returning it to his pocket.

'Does it do that every hour?' Mr Harris enquired in awe-stricken tones.

'Not during the night,' the Rector reassured him. 'One grows used to it. The clergy must perforce do so, for a vicarage or rectory is usually quite close to the church.'

'I suppose so.' Mr Harris seemed quite put off his stroke, and Lucinda, seeking to calm his nerves, said kindly, 'It no longer chimes the quarters, for the mechanism is very old and worn.'

'Quite so,' added the Rector, and smiled vaguely at the visitor. There was a pause, and then Mr Harris collected his wits and said, 'I fear I'm wasting a great deal of your time. I came to enquire whether you and Mrs Calvert, and Miss Calvert of course, would honour me by dining at Pinnacles tomorrow, if it would be convenient to you.'

The Rector looked at his daughter, who nodded slightly, signifying that he had no other dinner engagement, so he hastened to accept the invitation, at least for himself and Lucinda, although he added dubiously, 'I fear I cannot answer for my dear wife, for she enjoys delicate health, and it's difficult to forecast whether or not she will feel up to dining out when the time comes . . .' He tailed off, looking perplexed and embarrassed, but Mr Harris said obligingly that, if Mrs Calvert felt well enough to come, he would be delighted to see her, but if not, he would quite understand, and that he kept country hours when in the country, by which his prospective guests understood that they might expect dinner to be served at about six.

The Rector rang his bell as Mr Harris rose to take his departure, and Annie appeared to show him out properly.

'A pleasant gentleman,' the Rector observed before Mr Harris was altogether out of earshot. Lucinda waited until she heard the front door close before saying, 'Yes, indeed,' sounding less doubtful than she felt, for there was something about Mr Harris which made her feel uncomfortable.

'Frederick took to him, and I've always found him an excellent judge of character,' said her father, who was the more observant of tones of voice for being unable to see very well.

'One can hardly place overmuch reliance on a cat's judgment!' Lucinda objected. 'Besides, he detests poor Monsieur Roland!'

'Perhaps,' said her father pensively, 'he finds it difficult to tell a Royalist from a Bonapartist. I suppose all Frenchmen must smell much the same to a cat . . . I think your Mama is ringing again.'

Lucinda swallowed an impatient sigh and went upstairs to reply to the insistent tinkling of the little silver bell. She found her mother disposed languidly on a day-bed in the pleasant sunny room at the front of the house which she called her sitting-room, surrounded by half-read novels, half-done pieces of embroidery, a half-drunk cup of chocolate and a half-eaten biscuit.

'Did you ring, Mama?' Lucinda enquired, beginning to tidy the room.

'Several times, but no one answers,' Mrs Calvert said in a gentle, patient voice. 'I cannot think what Annie is doing, and why she cannot come!'

'She's very busy helping Cook with the jam,' Lucinda replied absently. Her tidying had taken her across the room to the window, and she stood looking out at the passing show. A cart had slipped part of its load as it came out of the ford across the mill-stream, and the idlers from the Black Swan down the street were helping the carter to reload it in a desultory fashion, watched by two children, a black and tan dog, a well-built man in black with a broad-brimmed hat, and a young clergyman with an armful of books. Mr Harris also appeared briefly in the picture, riding across it from right to left in the background on a fine bay horse, with a carriage-dog trotting alongside.

'What are you looking at?' Mrs Calvert asked fretfully.

'Just the activity in the street. I wonder you don't have your couch by the window, Mama. There's so much always going on just outside here, where the roadway widens in front of the church. The whole town must pass by in the course of a day!'

'I find no pleasure in watching ordinary people about their common pursuits,' Mrs Calvert said dismissively. 'And the carts grind so on the stones and make my head ache. Who was it came to the door a while back? Why am I not told what is going on?'

'I was about to tell you, Mama.' Lucinda turned from the window and looked at her mother, wishing that her health were better so that she could find more pleasure in life. She looked well, with a good colour, and was, indeed, still a pretty female, with not a grey thread in the auburn hair which Lucinda had inherited from her. Her clear, creamy skin was unblemished and still unlined, save for a slight frown, and she had beautiful green eyes, but no sparkle, no vivacity at all. She habitually looked weary, and came to life only in a real emergency.

'Well, then?' she prompted.

'It was a Mr Harris, the new owner of Pinnacles, come to ask us to dine with him tomorrow.'

Mrs Calvert's languid posture stiffened into something more alert, and she looked quite interested. 'What sort of a man is he?'

'A gentleman,' Lucinda replied. 'Quite young—well, thirtyish, I suppose—and tall. Rather thin. Er—well dressed. Fred liked him.'

'A fine recommendation,' Mrs Calvert said with a touch of acidity. 'He must be a paragon if the cat likes him! Where does he come from? What is his family? Has he any fortune? Is he married? Really, Lucinda—the man must have been here quite half an hour, and I suppose neither you nor your father thought to find out anything of importance about him.'

'He is unmarried, and has lived abroad for some years,' Lucinda supplied hastily, grasping at two facts which had emerged from her memory. 'He wishes to settle down in the country and—and make something of a neglected estate.'

'Abroad where?' Mrs Calvert prompted again. 'India, perhaps? Could he be a Nabob, do you think? He must have a fortune if he thinks to make anything of Pinnacles, for it's so shockingly run down. Is the house in any fit state for entertaining, do you suppose?'

'We shall see tomorrow,' Lucinda pointed out.

'Yes.' Mrs Calvert spoke absently, mentally reviewing her wardrobe and then Lucinda's. At this point in her thoughts, she suddenly became aware that Lucinda was wearing a faded muslin quite definitely in last year's mode and, to make matters worse, had a smear of some reddish sticky substance on her left cheek.

'Lucinda!' she exclaimed. 'You never received a gentleman looking like *that*! How could you? Whatever could he have thought!'

Lucinda glanced down at her frock and rubbed the jam on her cheek in a guilty fashion, hastily saying, 'I'm sure he didn't even notice, for you know how green and gloomy it is in Father's study,' but she was very much aware that those coolly observant eyes were not likely to have missed any detail, and she was vexed with herself, for, while by no means vain, she had no wish to be thought hoydenish or slatternly, least of all by a new-comer to the town.

'Who else is to dine tomorrow?' Mrs Calvert's mind darted busily in another direction. 'I suppose you didn't think to enquire? I thought as much,' in an exagger-atedly resigned tone. 'Really, Lucinda, you live in a dream, I believe! You're near twenty, and must think seriously of getting a husband before it's too late. Your father cannot live for ever, you know, and the spinster daughter of a deceased clergyman has very poor pros-pects for a comfortable life. My annuity dies with me, as your father's stipend does with him. Now, what do you plan to wear for this dinner?'

'You know I have but two evening gowns, Mama,' Lucinda replied, wishing that her mother would not keep pointing out the obvious. Far from living in a dream, she often worried about her future, in the intervals between dealing with more pressing problems.

'And whose fault is that, pray?' Mrs Calvert nagged on. 'There are quite half a dozen old gowns of my own which you could make over if you were not eternally sewing for ungrateful idlers who prefer to batten on their betters instead of turning to and finding themselves a proper means of earning a livelihood!'

'People do not choose to go into the Poorhouse, or to live in wretched hovels!' Lucinda was stung to retort. 'Helping the poor is a duty, and people expect the Rectory to take a lead in it.'

'Oh, you wretched girl! Now you presume to criticise your own mother for having such poor health as to be quite unable to take on any tasks in the parish. How could you be so unfeeling!'

'I don't criticise you, Mama,' Lucinda said firmly. 'I only said that people expect the Rectory to take a lead, and as you cannot, I must try to fill your place. Now, shall you come down to luncheon, or will Annie bring it up to you on a tray?'

'I shall come down.' Mrs Calvert dabbed at her eyes in a pathetic fashion with a tiny handkerchief, for she did indeed feel both unwell and depressed. 'Not that I feel at all up to it, but I do myself no good by lying here moping.' She leaned heavily on Lucinda's arm on the way downstairs, and was settled in her place in the dining-room only after sending Lucinda back upstairs to fetch another shawl and putting the Rector to the trouble of closing the window which was open and opening another instead.

When all was arranged to her satisfaction, she condescended to notice the unexpected guest at the table—her husband's curate, Mr Jones.

'Good day, Mr—er—,' she said somewhat frostily. 'I was not aware that we were to have the pleasure of your company at our table.'

'Good day, ma'am,' Mr Jones replied equably. 'I called to return some books which the Rector had lent me, and he was kind enough to invite me to take luncheon.'

'A glass of wine, Mrs Calvert?' the Rector enquired, the claret-jug poised in his hand.

'I do not care for claret in such warm weather. Is there no lemonade?'

'No, Mama. Lemons are become very scarce and dear,' Lucinda replied. She smiled across the table at Mr Jones as she passed him a dish of peas. He was, of course, the clergyman she had seen from the window a little earlier. Despite his name, he was not Welsh—at least, as he himself said, not recently, meaning that his forebears had left Wales many generations before—but he had the dark brown eyes and black hair common in that nation, and could speak in a passable imitation of the Welsh lilt when he chose. He was a handsome young man when he removed the steel-rimmed spectacles which he really only needed to wear for reading. He was saved from being too earnest by a quiet sense of humour, but his Celtic fervour for causes which caught at his heart or his imagination sometimes led the Rector to suspect him of Enthusiasm, a most undesirable quality in a clergyman. Look where it had led John Wesley!

'I'm sorry we have only cold cuts to offer you,' Lucinda remarked, passing on the dish of new potatoes to him. 'Cook is making jam today, with the last of the gooseberries. We had a very good crop this year, although Colonel Long's dogs ate a great many.'

'I didn't know dogs ate gooseberries.' Mr Jones removed his spectacles, put them in his pocket, and smiled at Lucinda.

'They do if they can get 'em!' the Rector said gloomily. 'The Colonel came to drink tea the other day, and let the dogs loose in the garden. Luckily they're a short-legged pair, so they were only able to reach the lower branches.'

Mr Jones lodged in the house of a respectable widow in Baker's Row, just across the road from the church, but his landlady was not a good cook. Lucinda suspected that the young man was often hungry, so she unobtrusively encouraged him to make a good meal by passing the dishes to him until the salad, peas and potatoes were all gone, and when Annie brought in a large gooseberry pie and set it before Lucinda to be served, somehow Mr Jones received almost twice as much as anyone else, a kindness which he acknowledged with a humorous twitch of his eyebrows and a little nod of thanks to his benefactress.

The conversation during the meal was chiefly of parish matters, and Mrs Calvert's one contribution—an enquiry addressed to her husband for more information about Mr Harris—produced no more than she had already learned from Lucinda. So she picked at her food in silence thereafter, seemingly deep in thought, and barely paused to bid Mr Jones farewell before retiring upstairs, murmuring that the warm weather was so exhausting, and leaving a trail of shawls for her daughter to collect and bring up to her room.

Lucinda, however, had better things to do. She draped the shawls on the banister, changed her frock, put on her bonnet, and left the Rectory with Mr Jones, taking with her a large basket, which he carried for her until they had walked up the churchyard path, through an arch and into the market square, where they parted company. As Lucinda took her basket from Mr Jones, she gave him the gallipot of gooseberry jam which was in it, bidding him carry it carefully, as it was still warm.

'You're very good to me, Miss Calvert!' he said earnestly, gazing down into her face. 'I'm most grateful to you.'

'It's from Cook,' Lucinda informed him kindly yet dampeningly. 'She's grateful to you for helping her brother to find work, and she's not much of a one with words, so she says her thanks with edibles.'

Mr Jones was not much put down by the news, for his heart was well hedged about with prudence and discretion. He requested Lucinda to convey his thanks to Cook, raised his low-crowned clerical hat politely and went on his way, carrying the warm gallipot before him like a jar of precious spikenard, lest it tip and make his gloves sticky.

Lucinda walked slowly across the market square, for it was a hot afternoon and the sun blazed down on the cobbles, so that they struck warm through her thin-soled slippers. There was no market today, and even the usual idlers seemed to have vanished in search of a cooler place, leaving the square deserted save for the cat Fred, who was on his stately way to call on a feline friend at the Wyvern on the west side of the square. He looked round when Lucinda called him, gave her a glacial stare, as if to indicate that he was not acquainted with her and did not care to be accosted by strange females, and then vanished with a sudden spring through an open sash window on the ground floor of the inn.

As Fred frequently disowned his friends when he met them out, Lucinda was not much distressed by the cut direct, but continued on her way to a large four-square red-brick house at the south-eastern corner of the square. There lived her friend Amaryllis Martin, whom she found seated under a shady tree in the garden, unpicking a rather grubby and uneven row of stitching in the seam of a shapeless calico garment which bore a paper label pinned to its front stating that it was a nightshirt.

'Oh, dear, Miss Enston again?' Lucinda enquired, catching sight of it as her friend rose to greet her. 'What are we to do with her, Amy? She does love to help, but nothing she makes is usable!'

'It depends what you mean by usable.' Amy's lively face dimpled. 'It would make a good cover for a haycock!'

'The rain would get in at the neck,' Lucinda pointed out, sitting down at the table on which were several finished and folded garments, and taking her own work out of her basket.

Amy resumed her unpicking, and the two young ladies were silent for a few moments, presenting a charming picture amid the damask roses, jasmine, mignonette and lilies which were all filling the hot afternoon with heady scent. Amy Martin was a dark-haired girl with merry brown eyes and a brown complexion, a tip-tilted nose and a wide mouth which always looked as if it were about to smile if it was not actually doing so. She and Lucinda had been friends for many years and spent much of their time together, usually sewing, for they were the prime movers in a circle of local ladies who kept the poor people of the parish, both in and out of the Poorhouse, supplied with decent clothing, mostly second-hand, but new when they had any cloth to make it.

'So!' said Amy presently. 'Do you mean to keep your

news a secret, or are you waiting to hear mine first?'

'What news?' Lucinda looked up from her sewing. 'Oh, I suppose you mean Mr Harris.'

'Well, according to the Fount of All Knowledge, Mr Harris was seen to call at the Rectory this morning, followed shortly by Mr Jones, who stayed to luncheon. Monsieur Roland, on the other hand, approached your door, but changed his mind and went away again.'

'I can't imagine how Miss Enston manages it!' Lucinda exclaimed. 'She must spend half her time watching other people, and the other half telling someone what she has seen. What did she have to say about Mr Harris?'

'Very little, as she's not managed to speak to him yet, although she said she's exchanged a few words with his groom, only eliciting the information that the gentleman's a good judge of horseflesh. What did you think of him?'

Lucinda unconsciously stopped sewing and sat still, staring unseeingly before her and thinking for a few moments before replying. 'I'm not sure. He seems a pleasant gentleman, and equable in disposition. Fred gave him a mouse, and even that didn't appear to rattle him overmuch, and when Father assumed he'd come to put up the banns, he took it with good humour. I do wish he would buy a new pair of spectacles!'

Amy laughed. 'And whom did your father think was to be the bride?'

'Me!' Lucinda replied, smiling. 'Only Father thought he was Will Plomer, you see, and that I was Jenny Briggs, his intended! Mr Harris invited us to dine with him tomorrow, and even Mama has decided to go, for she can't resist seeing what he has made of the house.'

'My mother, too. He called here earlier, and Mama put him to the question in her best Leading Counsel manner.' (Amy's father was the town's solicitor.) 'But she failed to discover any more of him than the fact that he has been abroad a great deal, and he means to make something of the Pinnacles estates.'

'That's all he told us. How odd!' Lucinda commented. 'Not that Father or I questioned him, exactly. By the time one has sorted out the table of forbidden degrees, and ascertained whether one of Fred's offerings is a field mouse or a house mouse, there's not much of a morning call left! He didn't say that he'd invited anyone else to dine—do you think there will be a large party?'

'He said something about Colonel and Mrs Long, and I suppose there will have to be one odd gentleman to even the numbers. Mama did manage to discover that Mr Harris is a bachelor, so, of course, she's been weaving plots ever since, for she calculates that he must be worth quite fifteen thousand pounds a year to do something with the Pinnacles land.'

'My Mama didn't put a figure to it, but her thoughts followed the same lines.' Lucinda's face clouded, and she went on sadly, 'I know she's only thinking of my future, but I do dislike the way she views every bachelor we meet as a possible husband for me! I don't wish to be auctioned off to the highest bidder.'

'Nor I.' For once, Amy was not smiling, but looked quite sad. 'It's not as important for me to marry a wealthy man, for Papa can give me a good portion, but if I follow my inclination, I expect they'll do their best to persuade me to change my mind.'

'Why, Amy! Have you someone in mind? You've never said!' Lucinda was startled.

Amy gave an odd little grimace, and said reluctantly, 'Well, I sometimes think I should like . . . Oh, but he doesn't take the least notice of me. I expect he thinks me giddy and light-minded, if he ever notices me at all! Perhaps Mr Harris will invite Captain Bridges for tomorrow night. How will that please you?'

'Oh, well enough, but I think I should prefer Monsieur Roland,' Lucinda replied, accepting the change of subject as a warning-off from something which her friend did not wish to discuss.

'I don't expect he knows Monsieur Roland yet,' Amy pointed out. 'Although he'll soon meet him when he starts to dine about the town. I think Monsieur Roland must be our most popular single man—I suppose it's his French charm and his little air of mystery. Do you think he really is a nobleman incognito?'

'Perhaps.' Lucinda shrugged. 'He's never actually said so, only that he does not care to use his real name while he's a refugee, for the sake of others still in France. Poor man—he must find it tedious, waiting for France to be free so that he can return there—it must be quite fifteen or sixteen years that he's been an exile. He's very melancholy about it at times, and says he feels that he's no nearer going home than he was when he first came to England! I come upon him in the church sometimes, just sitting there quietly and looking so sad.'

'I thought he was Catholic?'

'So he is, but there's no Catholic church hereabouts for him to go to, so what is he to do? Father doesn't mind—he says our church was Catholic before the Reformation, and he'd raise no objection to a Hottentot going in there, provided he was quietly-behaved and reverent.'

'Now don't go falling in love with the man, I beg you!' Amy wagged a finger. 'We can't have the daughter of a clergyman of the Established Church marrying a French Catholic, and a practically penniless *émigré* at that!'

'No.' Lucinda sounded a little regretful. 'I suppose it's quite out of the question, although he's very handsome and charming . . . I expect it will be Captain Bridges, as you say, for he's the Colonel's aide-de-camp, and it seems an obvious choice.'

'For you to marry, do you mean?' Amy enquired mischievously.

'No, for Mr Harris to invite to dinner; although I suppose Mama would favour him for the other, for he's quite rich and well connected, you know. His father is a baronet, his uncle a bishop, and his elder brother an archdeacon. You said something about news,' Lucinda recollected. 'Was there something else?'

'I'm afraid there is—bad news,' Amy said with regret. 'Papa doesn't wish me to go to Cob End any more.'

'Oh, but why not?' cried Lucinda. 'Surely he doesn't think those poor souls would do you any harm?'

'I don't believe it's that. Partly it's because their landlord, Mr Marshall, is one of Papa's clients, and he thinks that my going there might offend him, and partly it's because he thinks I might take some illness from them, with their water-supply being so scant and dirty, and the hot weather . . . I'm sorry, Lucy. I tried hard to persuade him to relent, but it was no use.'

'Never mind.' Lucinda tried to keep the disappointment out of her voice, for she had counted on Amy's support in her frequent visits to the poorest of her father's parishoners. 'I shall have to go by myself, or perhaps Job, our stable-lad, will come with me sometimes, if he can be spared.'

'I hope so, for I don't like to think of you toiling up the hill with heavy baskets,' Amy said doubtfully. 'And you can never be sure what you'll find when you arrive!'

CHAPTER TWO

MR HARRIS was kind enough to send his groom in the morning to enquire if he should instruct his coachman to fetch the Rectory party, and the Rector replied that he was obliged to Mr Harris, but that he had his own carriage. It was old and rather shabby, despite Job's efforts in washing and polishing, but quite serviceable, and it conveyed Mr and Mrs Calvert and Lucinda towards Pinnacles in good time for the dinner-party.

Woodham was a small town in those days, little more than a main street, which ran from the bridge across the river, past the powder-mill and up to the church, then made a dog-leg round the churchyard to the market square, calling itself West Street up to that point, then changed its name to East Street to continue for a few hundred yards to the end of the town. It then became Forest Lane and went through the fields and up the hill until it vanished into the Forest and the wide world beyond. Just before it entered the trees, it passed Pinnacles on the left, set back about half a mile and standing sideways to the road, facing down the hill towards the town, the military camp to the north, and the river, with the next county beyond.

Mr and Mrs Calvert talked in a desultory fashion (Mrs Calvert being already quite worn down with the effort of dressing) about visits to Pinnacles in the old days, when Sir Robert Hook the elder was still alive and well. But

Lucinda had never been there before, although she had often walked along the footpath just below the terraced gardens of the house, and wondered what it was like inside, so she was looking forward to finding out.

She had done her best to please her mother and make the best of herself by putting on the better of her two evening gowns—a pale green shot silk with tiny puffed sleeves, the fashionable high waist and a modest *décolletée*, trimmed with darker green ribbons stitched from waist to hem, two at the front and two at the back. Her long white kid gloves were new and rather tight, and she had swept up her auburn curls with a scarf made out of a spare piece of the fabric of her gown.

Mrs Calvert wore a dove grey velvet tunic over a darker grey taffeta skirt, and a blue velvet turban trimmed with a little marabou, and Mr Calvert was, of course, in his sober clerical black, with his white parson's wig, which he much disliked and seldom managed to keep on straight. He had been persuaded to allow Lucinda to give his spectacles a good wash, and could see rather better than usual.

'Why!' he exclaimed as they drew near the gates of Pinnacles. 'What's that in the field by the lodge? Piles of bricks? Several loads, I believe! And timber! Mr Harris must mean to build something. I wonder what it can be.'

'A new lodge, perhaps,' Mrs Calvert replied in an uninterested tone. 'I believe that is the Martins' carriage turned in ahead of us. We are not to be the only guests, then.'

Lucinda, who had forgotten to pass on the information she had learned from Amy Martin, said quietly, 'Colonel and Mrs Long are also invited, I believe.'

'There, you see,' exclaimed Mrs Calvert. 'Really, Mr Calvert, you should have called on Mr Harris, and not put him to the embarrassment of having to make the first move.'

'I was not aware that he'd come into residence,' the Rector replied mildly, 'or I would certainly have called.'

'Well, the Longs and the Martins must have known, and called, or how do they come to be dining here?' his wife said tartly. 'I do think they might have let us know!'

'I believe he called on Mrs Martin as he did upon us,' Lucinda put in. 'Why, even Miss Enston didn't mention that Mr Harris had come, so I'm sure no one else knew!'

The state of the land belonging to Pinnacles was well known to Lucinda from her frequent passage across the estate on her way to Cob End, but it was a long time since either of her parents had been there, and there were frequent exclamations at the encroaching brambles, rampant thistles and other signs of neglect as the carriage rolled along the drive between the fields. The area near the house was populated by a dozen donkeys, who were hardly visible amid the tall grass.

'Bless my soul!' exclaimed the Rector. 'Those are donkeys, are they not? I thought for a moment they were rabbits, for I could only see their ears. They must find it hard to eat thistles taller than themselves!'

Lucinda was tempted to say that they must think themselves in Paradise, but her father did not always appreciate jokes with religious connotations, so she refrained.

The house had been visible for some time, gradually coming nearer, but it looked much as it had always done—an attractive red-brick building of Jacobean style, with large windows and ornamental chimneys, and elaborate gable-ends decorated with the terracotta pinnacles which gave the house its name, each topped by a once-gilded weathervane. Rust and neglect, however, had caused the vanes to disagree with one another, and, according to them, the wind was blowing from almost every point of the compass at once.

The carriage rumbled through an archway in a high brick wall and moved slowly along the side of the house, then round the corner to the front, which faced towards the Forest. Here were signs that much work had been done, for the gravel drive was weeded and raked, the flower-beds neatly planted, the trees and shrubs trimmed, the grass cut and rolled, the windows repaired and cleaned, the paintwork gleamingly fresh, and at least half a dozen men and boys were at work weeding and trimming round the beds.

Inside the house, everything was new. In fact, Lucinda felt a little disorientated at first, for the outside of the house was typical of the early seventeenth century while the inside was completely up to date, apart from the windows. The walls were either painted in fashionable pastel colours or covered with light damasks, the ceilings were plastered in the latest Grecian designs, and the furniture was elegantly modern, some in the new Egyptian style, but most owing more to the designs of Mr Adam, whose hand was also apparent in the chimney-pieces.

Mr Harris received his guests in a very handsome drawing-room, which could really claim to be called a salon, for it was a large double cube with a grand coved alcove across one end. The walls were covered with pale gold fabric woven in a design of leafy swags, and hung with fine pictures, mostly landscapes. The design of the very large carpet was mirrored in the plasterwork of the ceiling, and swags like those on the walls were carved on the top rails of the padded chairs and sofas. Three very large windows in the long wall opposite the door stood open on to the top terrace of the garden, and were framed by a clever draping of pelmets and curtains which matched the walls.

Mr and Mrs Martin and Amy were already seated and looking quite at home, but they rose to greet the new-comers. Mrs Martin looked a trifle dowdy in a dark purple satin low-waisted round-gown and an elaborate lace cap, but Mr Martin had a fashionable puce brocade waistcoat under his sober lawyer's black coat. Amy was a pretty picture in embroidered white muslin, with silver ribbons threaded through her dark curls and laced into her sandals.

The Longs arrived soon after, the Colonel a fine florid-faced figure in his scarlet coat, and his wife, also florid-faced, rather stout in pale blue taffeta of the very latest fashion. They were accompanied by Captain Bridges, a picture-book hero from his polished Hessians to the dark curls six feet above them. His face was classically Grecian, his red coat fitted his broad shoulders to perfection, he was well-mannered, graceful in his compliments and his dancing, courteous even to plain or elderly females, deferent to his superiors without over-doing it, undoubtedly brave (he wore both the Honour-able East India Company's medal and the Turkish Order of the Crescent for the Egyptian Campaign of 1801) and reasonably modest. Most of the young ladies in the town were more or less in love with him, but he seemed to divide his attention fairly equally between Lucinda and Amy, both of whom quite liked him.

This, apparently, was the full complement of guests. As they were all acquainted, and saw each other several times a week, there was no shortage of conversation, and Mr Harris was able to stand before his elegant marble chimney-piece, sipping his wine and observing them all with a faint smile, which Lucinda, on catching sight of it, thought a little sardonic.

'Why, Mr Harris!' she said, moving across to him. 'How ill-mannered you must think us all, chattering among ourselves and not including you in our talk.'

'Not at all, Miss Calvert,' he replied, the smile broadening. 'I prefer to listen rather than to talk. The day is very warm again, is it not? Do you find it too hot in here? All the windows which will open are open, but there seems to be little current of air.'

'No doubt Mama will manage to detect a draught if anyone should wish for one,' Lucinda replied ruefully, then regretted her words, for she did not wish to appear disloyal to her mother.

'How is the redoubtable Fred?' their host enquired. 'Has he any offspring? We're a little bothered by small rodents in parts of the house, and a good mouser would be most welcome—In fact, an urgent need!'

'Fred is quite well, thank you. I believe that one of his daughters might be obtainable, if a queen would do, or would you prefer a tom?'

'I've no preference, provided the animal catches mice!' was the grave reply. 'Would you be so kind as to act as my agent in the matter? I'm willing to pay the animal's weight in corn, or whatever is the going rate these days.'

'I'll see what I can do,' Lucinda promised. She had been covertly eyeing Mr Harris's costume, which was deceptively simple, but fitted to perfection. His coat was blue, his waistcoat plain white, his pantaloons plain black, his pumps made even Captain Bridges's Hessians look dull, and his cravat was a masterpiece. She thought that he would probably have carried his head somewhat proudly without the restriction of the stiff collar, but she charitably blamed it for his fashion of looking down his nose in such a haughty manner.

'Are you a Corinthian?' she asked cautiously.

'In what sense?' His smile broadened still more to reveal a row of even, white teeth. 'I'm not a rake-hell, if you meant that, but if it's the new definition—a sportsman, or a man who prefers his linen clean and his coats well tailored—I might make a modest claim to some pretensions in that direction. I don't mix in the Ton, though.'

'Do you spend much time in London?' Lucinda thought he had given her a sufficient opening for the question.

'As little as possible. I've been abroad a great deal in recent years.'

'In India?' She felt she must pry a little more in order to satisfy her mother.

'Not if I can avoid it. Too hot.'

Amy, intrigued and perhaps a little envious at seeing Lucinda engaged in conversation with the mysterious newcomer, had drifted closer, and was drawn into the conversation by Mr Harris, who asked her solemnly, 'Are you come to join the inquisition, Miss Martin? Your friend is endeavouring to discover whether or not I'm a Nabob.'

'And are you?' Amy asked artlessly, turning wide brown eyes upon him in a fashion which she had found usually melted the hearts of gentlemen of any age.

'I assure you, Miss Martin,' he replied gravely, laying his hand on his heart, 'I was never an official in the government of the Great Mogul. Now, I believe my butler is endeavouring to catch my eye, if you'll excuse me . . .'

He slipped neatly between the two young ladies, with a smile for each, and left them looking puzzled.

'I suppose that's what a Nabob was originally,' said Lucinda doubtfully, 'but he must know that it now means a man who has made his fortune in India, unless he's been abroad so long he's forgotten . . .'

Further speculation was ended by the announcement that dinner was served, and the guests filed two by two into the dining-room, Mr Harris taking in Mrs Calvert, the Rector with Mrs Long, the Colonel with Mrs Martin, Mr Martin with Lucinda, and Captain Bridges with Amy. At the table, Lucinda found herself between Mr Martin and Captain Bridges, with Amy next and Mr Harris beyond her.

The dining-room, surprisingly, had not been modernised. Its walls were panelled with elaborately-carved oak, the fireplace was large enough to take a whole tree-trunk (but was now occupied by a large vase of flowers), and the furniture was old, dark and heavy, the chairlegs swelling into bulbous and gouty-looking excrescences as did also some part of the underpinnings of the table, for Lucinda stubbed her toe on one of them, but could not see it as the snowy linen tablecloth concealed it from her.

Two massive court-cupboards against the wall showed off a fine display of silver, and there was more silver, sparkling crystal and elegant china on the table. The food was delicious, varied and well chosen, for the soup was iced, the dishes nearly all light, cold and summery, with a choice of roasts and hot vegetables for those who expected a hot meal, regardless of the weather, and there were ices, syllabub, strawberries and cream to follow, then a variety of cheeses and the most luscious dessert fruits Lucinda had ever seen—peaches, nectarines, grapes and oranges.

The wines were apparently very good too, for Colonel Long, who was something of a connoisseur, complimented Mr Harris on his wine-merchant, at which Mr Harris's ironic smile appeared as he replied, 'I fear most of this has never seen a bonded warehouse!'

'*He must mean the wine is smuggled!*' Lucinda thought, surprised that he should already be buying from the local smugglers when he had only just arrived, until it occurred to her that he might have brought his cellar with him from—from wherever he had come. No one, of course, looked in the least shocked to discover that their wine had not paid excise duty, for even Mr Martin and the Rector had their mysterious little barrels left in the garden in the dead of night, and paid surprisingly large bills to the blacksmith for sundry nails and hinges and brackets, and the ladies could hardly have allowed their servants to drink tea if they had bought all of it from the grocer's shop in the town.

After dinner, the ladies withdrew to the salon to drink tea and coffee, and were soon joined by the gentlemen. The older members of the party then settled to conversation and whist, but the two young ladies and Captain Bridges elected to go with Mr Harris for a stroll in the garden to see how it had been restored, for it was oppressively hot indoors now that the candles had been brought, and the summer evening outside looked particularly inviting.

Lucinda, of course, was admonished by her mother to take a shawl, but, once outside, she hung it over the balustrade of the terrace, meaning to collect it on her return.

The garden at the back of the house descended in three broad terraces, each bounded by an ornamental stone balustrade, with twin flights of steps down to the next level. The terraces were planted with beds of roses and other flowers, little trees in tubs, and larger trees at the sides, and had stone-paved paths meandering about, with statues and seats and urns placed here and there. The air was full of the scent of roses, and the drowsy hum of bees was the only sound, apart from the occasional distant roar of a donkey.

They wandered about the terraces for some time, looking at the flowers and admiring the statues, one of which, a Hermes, bore a distinct resemblance to Captain Bridges—in the face, at least, for his uniform precluded any comparison extending lower than his leather stock. Presently Amy sat down on a convenient seat to remove a stone from her sandal and Captain Bridges remained to assist her, while Lucinda strolled on with Mr Harris and descended the steps to the lowest terrace.

From the balustrade, when they reached it, they had a fine view over the fields to the town, a flock of red roofs clustering round the four-square white stone tower of the church. Beyond the town, the river meandered gently through the meadows, its navigation cut running straight and businesslike this side of it, and both were cut across by the dusty white road on its way to the next county on the far side of the valley, where the ground rose, thickly wooded, until a distant church spire caught the sun on the skyline, level with where they were standing.

Lucinda looked along to her right, to where the wooden barrack-blocks of the army camp lay in neat ranks on the lower fields, above the winter flood-level, with the tiny splash of colour of a Union flag flying from a white pole in the midst of them. It was an unpleasant reminder that this peaceful-looking country had been at war, with one short interval, for fourteen years, and the reminder was suddenly reinforced by a loud bang, which echoed back from the Forest behind them like a clap of thunder, followed by an outburst of flapping wings as startled birds shot into the air in all directions.

'What was that?' exclaimed Mr Harris.

'It was an explosion at the powder-mill,' Lucinda

replied, pointing. 'There, you see? Those big, dark buildings between the town and the river. I don't think it's anything much, for there's no smoke. Sometimes they explode some powder to test it, and I expect that's what they were doing this time, for the workmen will have gone home by now.'

'But sometimes it's not done a'purpose?' Mr Harris asked grimly.

'No. Unfortunately, sometimes, there are bad accidents, for it's dangerous stuff to handle. There were seven men killed last year when one of the corning-houses blew up. One body was never found.'

'Surely they take precautions?'

'Yes, very stringent ones! Any man who goes into the mill with metal about him is dismissed at once, and they're all most careful—for their life's sake, not for fear of dismissal!—but it takes very little to set it off—too much or too little of one ingredient, or something in the weather. Once, one of the stores was struck by lightning . . . I still dream of it occasionally!'

Lucinda shuddered, and Mr Harris put a hand lightly on her shoulder. 'I suppose, through your father's position, you must hear much of the sadness of life in this town,' he said softly. 'Why do men work there, if it's so dangerous?'

'It's well paid, and many of them take pride in it, for it's skilled work, as well as dangerous. There's a certain element of patriotism, too, especially with England at war. I think, too, that most men enjoy a little danger, don't you? I mean—why else do they join the army or the navy?'

'Some have no choice,' Mr Harris replied grimly. He did not need to enlarge on the subject of crimping-houses, unscrupulous recruiting sergeants or press-gangs.

'But many are volunteers?'

At that moment the church bells began to ring, rag-gedly and individually at first, but gradually gaining momentum and settling into their proper order.

'Is that an alarum, because of the explosion?' Mr Harris asked, removing his hand from Lucinda's shoul-der and tensing himself as if he meant to vault over the balustrade and run down the hill to the town.

'No, they'd ring backwards if it was that! It's only the ringers ringing-up for their practice,' Lucinda explained. 'It's always on Thursday evening.'

'Backwards? How do they ring backwards?'

'Up the scale, instead of down.'

The bells settled into their strokes for a few minutes, as they listened, and then stopped.

'They're all rung up now,' Lucinda said. 'Now they'll ring plain rounds a few times. Up in the ringing chamber, they'll be standing ready while the Captain tells them which system they're going to ring, and checks that they all know the pattern, and then the treble will look round to see they're all ready, and he'll say, "Faith's going" as he pulls the rope, then "She's gone" as he feels the bell start to swing, and the others will follow in turn.'

Even as she finished speaking, the bells rang out, tumbling down the scale, Faith, Hope and Charity, James and John, Raphael, Michael and Gabriel.

'Now,' Lucinda continued, 'in a few minutes, the Cap-tain will call "Bob!" and they'll go into their changes.'

'Who is Faith?' Mr Harris asked, after listening for a while to the brazen voices twisting and turning through the pattern, bobbing, hunting up, weaving in sound across the valley.

Lucinda told him the names of the bells. 'Faith is the treble—the smallest, James and John are the chime bells, and Gabriel, the tenor, is the biggest. He sounds the hours, and is the passing bell, for Gabriel is the Guardian of Souls.'

'Which is it that rings so early in the morning?' Mr Harris was very interested in what was, for him, a new subject.

'That's usually Michael—the apprentice bell, to tell the townspeople when to get up, but sometimes Mr Gibbs, the sexton, rings one of the others for a change.'

'And who wakes him, to be up the tower by six in the morning, I wonder? I'll admit that I don't stir myself until seven!' Mr Harris sounded quite ashamed, but Lucinda thought that most wealthy landowners would probably lie abed much later than that.

'Would the ringers let me watch them one evening, do you think?' he asked. He was moving a forefinger about as if counting something in the air before him, but Lucinda realised that he was trying to follow the course of one bell.

'I'm sure they would. Will Plomer, the blacksmith, is their Captain. If you ask him, he'll tell you when you may go up the tower.' She wondered how he would react to the idea of asking permission of a mere blacksmith, but he seemed to appreciate that there was nothing 'mere' about such an important person, for he said, 'Ah, yes—Mr Plomer, the man who wishes to be married! A skilled craftsman, I hear, with a good knowledge of horses' hooves.'

The sun was sliding down to the horizon now, the western sky was crimson with promise for another fine day on the morrow, and the thistles in the field below the balustrade shone as if gilded in the evening light. Lucinda and Mr Harris leaned side by side upon the balustrade, watching the homing birds and listening to the bells in companionable silence.

'Look, a rabbit!' Mr Harris whispered, pointing. A white scut bobbed across the field and vanished into the hedge.

'There are plenty of rabbits.' Lucinda sounded puzzled. 'Too many, the farmers say.'

'Not necessarily.' Mr Harris seemed to be searching the field for more rabbits. 'Yes—two over there, and another—see, there he goes! This land has been enclosed for a long time, I believe?'

'Nearly a hundred years. And my father thinks that these fields on the edge of the Forest—intakes, he calls them—are much older than that. The hedges are very strong and thick, and have quite large trees in them. Oh, look!' Lucinda seized Mr Harris's arm in an unconsciously tight grip and sank her voice to a whisper. 'Look, a deer!'

'Yes. I was told that there are only a few left in the Forest, yet we've had some difficulty in persuading at least a score that the kitchen gardens are not planted for their benefit!' His voice softened as he added, 'But they're beautiful creatures.'

'Ah, here they are!' exclaimed Captain Bridges from behind them, appearing round a lilac bush with Amy beside him. The deer gave a startled jump and disappeared rapidly, and Lucinda also jumped, released Mr Harris's arm, and backed away from him, feeling unaccountably confused and embarrassed as she realised how close to him she had been standing.

'We were watching the real owners of my fields,' Mr Harris said lightly. 'Shall we return to the house? I fear I've been neglecting my other guests quite shamefully, and the midges are beginning to bite.'

As they walked slowly back across the rising terraces, Amy remarked how admirably the gardens had been restored. 'Captain Bridges and I were amazed to see how quickly you've had everything put to rights. Why, you've been here only a week or two, yet everything is already quite perfect.'

'I've been in residence for just a week, but the workmen and gardeners have been busy these past three months,' he replied. 'A positive army of them, in fact! Most of them have returned to London now, and the rest will soon follow. I intend to employ local people, apart from the upper servants.'

'I'm very glad to hear it,' said Amy. 'There are several good people hereabouts in need of work. Isn't it strange—we had no idea down in the town that so much was being done here, for the house and gardens can hardly be seen, even from the path that runs just below the terraces.'

'Oh, yes—that path.' Mr Harris seemed interested. 'It appears to come up through the fields and then go across below the gardens, skirting the edge of the Forest towards the north, and eventually leaving my land by a stile in the boundary hedge. Where does it go then, and who uses it? I've not seen anyone on it, but I've not had it under continuous observation.'

'It used to go to Forest House, but when Mr Marshall bought the estate he had the house pulled down, and now the path goes only to Cob End, and the poor folk there have little need to go down to the town, for they've no money to spend there,' Amy informed him. 'Miss Calvert and I use it quite often, but hardly anyone else.'

'Someone else uses it, for I've seen hoof-marks . . .' Lucinda began, then broke off, recalling that there was a particular group of people who might well use the path to go from the Forest to the town without using the road, and they were not a subject for idle talk. 'You don't intend to close it, I hope?' she substituted for what she might have been about to say.

'Of course not, if it's used, Miss Calvert. In any case, I believe it's a right of way.' Mr Harris appeared not to have heard the first part of Lucinda's speech.

'I use it myself occasionally,' Captain Bridges volunteered. 'I expect they were my hoof-marks you saw. When I'm riding, I often cut across Mr Marshall's land from the camp and then follow the Selvedge—the path under discussion—and so down to the town for a circular ride, returning to the camp along the river, with firm footing all the way.'

'There must be many pleasant rides in the vicinity,' Mr Harris observed. 'Do you ride, ladies?'

'Sometimes,' Amy replied for both. 'At least, I do, when Father's not using his mare, but Lucinda—Miss Calvert—has no mount now, though she used to ride quite often.'

There was a pause as Mr Harris turned to Lucinda in the twilight, an unspoken question hovering in the air.

'I had an old pony,' she said reluctantly, 'but he died.' She did not add that she could not ask her father for the money he could ill afford for another horse.

'Then you must both allow me to find you mounts,' Mr Harris said. 'I keep a good stable, and I'd be grateful to you if you would help me to keep the cattle exercised, and show me something of the countryside.'

They were mounting the last flight of steps as he spoke, and had entered the house before either of the young ladies could reply. There was no opportunity after that, for Mr Harris went at once to slip easily into the conversation of the older folk, who were having a comfortable chat. Presently he enquired if anyone would care to try his new pianoforte, which stood in the alcove at the end of the room.

'My daughter plays quite well.' Mrs Martin seized upon the chance to show off one of Amy's accomplishments—'I'm sure she will oblige . . .'

'But Mama! I've not brought any music,' she protested quietly.

'There's music as well,' Mr Harris assured her. 'Pray favour us with a tune, Miss Martin? I'm sure everyone would like to hear you play.'

He conducted Amy to the pianoforte, which was a very pretty one, its satinwood case inlaid with swags of leaves in fruitwood to match the rest of the room. She turned over the brand new sheet-music and found some pieces she knew, then settled herself on the stool and tried a preliminary run over the keys.

'Oh, what a beautiful tone!' she exclaimed, her reluctance giving way to pleasure, and played quite happily (and reasonably well) for a while, Captain Bridges turning over for her and leaning admiringly against the instrument in between.

Lucinda felt a little despondent, for she was unable to play, never having had a pianoforte on which to learn, and she was also a trifle miffed with Captain Bridges, who seemed this evening to be showing a decided preference for Amy, although he had always in the past divided his attention equally between the two friends.

'Would Miss Calvert care to favour us with a tune?' Mr Harris asked smilingly, as the applause died down at the end of Amy's performance.

'Miss Calvert doesn't play,' Amy said quickly, kindly saving Lucinda the embarrassment of admitting it herself. 'But she sings.'

'Not very well!' Lucinda added in a low, nervous voice, suddenly convinced that Mr Harris must be used to hearing the finest singers in the world and would find her own small talent uninspiring, if not risible.

'Nonsense, Lucy!' The Rector, who had apparently been in a gentle doze, roused himself to protest in positive tones. 'You sing very well! Not a blackbird or a nightingale, it's true, but a tuneful little wren, at least.'

Lucinda looked up at Mr Harris with a mixture of chagrin and amusement at this rather two-edged recommendation, and met those coolly considering grey eyes, which suddenly twinkled a little as if they shared a private joke. At his wordless invitation, she went to consult with Amy over the pile of music.

'You wretched traitress!' she murmured to her friend.

'I thought you would wish to share the burden!' Amy replied mischievously. 'Here's one you know.'

'I think it's the only one.' Lucinda was both regretful and relieved, for it seemed ungracious to insist on singing only one song, yet she was not enough of a singer to wish to attempt something unfamiliar before an audience. She took up her stance within the curve of the pianoforte, took a few breaths while bowing slightly in acknowledgment of the little flurry of hand-clapping, and then launched into 'The Sweet Nightingale'.

It was a pretty, lilting tune, and her voice, although light in tone and limited in volume, was sufficient to do it justice. Captain Bridges cleared his throat and kindly provided a supportive second in the choruses in a pleasant baritone, and she got through it pretty well in her own estimation, and more than that, according to her audience.

To her relief, a couple of unobtrusively efficient footmen then brought in refreshment in the form of dainty sandwiches, more tea and coffee, or brandy for those of the gentlemen who preferred it. The Rector and Colonel Long exchanged significant glances after tasting the spirit, for it was of extraordinary quality.

A little later, Mr Harris begged his guests' indulgence to join him in a glass of champagne, which caused a mild sensation, as it was not a beverage customarily served in Woodham—in fact, only the Military and Mr Martin had ever tasted it before.

It was served in fine crystal flutes, and when everyone had a full glass, the ladies sniffing cautiously at the unfamiliar bubbly liquid, Mr Harris addressed a few words to them.

'I don't intend to weary you with a long speech,' he began, standing very upright before his fine marble chimney-piece. 'But I must thank you all for coming to my house this evening, despite my breach of custom in calling on you before you had had any opportunity to call on me, and for being so welcoming and kindly to a newcomer in your midst. I've been looking forward with keen anticipation to settling down in the country, and considered myself very fortunate in finding this house, which exactly fits the dream I've cherished for several years, and now I find that, beyond all I had hoped for in coming here, I'm also to be blessed with a circle of acquaintances for whom I have already formed an affection. I look forward to many happy evenings as pleasant as this one has been for me, and, I hope, for you.'

He was interrupted at this point by murmurs of agreement from his audience, and a hearty 'Hear, hear!' from the Colonel.

'Thank you for your approval. Now, may I give you a toast—to the people of Woodham, both native, long-resident, and new-come! Ladies and gentlemen—Ourselves!'

Lucinda echoed the toast, as did everyone else, then sipped her wine cautiously. It tasted, she thought, much like a very cold cider, and the bubbles gave an odd sensation at the back of her nose. A second taste made her realise that it was much better than cider, for it had a delicate, almost flower-like, flavour.

'Nectar!' Amy whispered. 'Just as I imagine the nectar of the Gods must taste!'

Lucinda agreed, and was not reluctant to allow her glass to be refilled by one of the footmen, but she decided, half-way through the second glass, that the wine was very heady, and it would be best not to drink too much of it.

On the way home, after bidding Mr Harris an unusually effusive good night, Mrs Calvert reverted to her more usual self and complained of feeling excessively tired, but she rallied sufficiently to enquire what Lucinda had managed to discover about their host.

'Why, nothing, Mama!' Lucinda was rather surprised to realise that this was so.

'But you were out in the garden an age! What on earth did you talk about?' Mrs Calvert demanded querulously.

Lucinda thought for a moment, and then replied, 'Well, the garden, of course, and the powder-mill, and—er—bell-ringing, and—let me see—rabbits, and enclosures, and—and footpaths. Oh, and riding.' She was surprised to find that she could recall almost every word of the conversation, and she felt her cheeks burn in the darkness of the carriage as she remembered how she had seized Mr Harris's arm when the deer appeared.

'But surely you discovered where he comes from, or what he means to build by the lodge?' Mrs Calvert exclaimed, patently bitterly disappointed in her daughter.

'My dear, she could hardly put our host to the question about his origins or intentions!' the Rector protested mildly. 'Did you not think the house very fine? The rooms seemed to me to be quite beautiful.'

The change of subject gave meat for conversation for the rest of the way home, for Mrs Calvert was pleased to give a detailed opinion of everything she had observed in the decorations and furnishing of Pinnacles, and very little had escaped her attention.

It was only as Lucinda was about to climb into bed that she recollected her shawl, left hanging on the balustrade of Mr Harris's terrace.

CHAPTER THREE

FRIDAY WAS always a busy day for Lucinda, as she usually spent the morning (and sometimes the afternoon as well) carrying out one of the duties expected of a parson's wife—visiting the old and the sick. Mrs Calvert rarely felt well enough to join in this, but Lucinda, taking it on in her mother's place as a matter of course, found a certain satisfaction in doing it.

Nevertheless, it was hard work. She set off early with her basket full of bottles of herbal mixtures, jars of broth, screws of tea, eggs, little gallipots of jam, or whatever else the Rectory kitchen could spare, and went from one home to another, staying perhaps ten minutes or even half an hour at each, usually finding that the room occupied by the sick person had its windows tightly closed, and sometimes a fire burning as well, for everyone knew that fresh air was fatal, and a good fire essential to recovery.

What with the heat, the stuffiness, the strong smell of unwashed bodies and boiled cabbage, and the difficulty of shouted conversations with the elderly and deaf, she was usually limp and exhausted by the time she reached home.

This morning was no exception. The hot weather continued, and it was well past half-past eleven as she walked slowly down the churchyard path with her empty basket, her hair sticking in damp curls to her head under her straw bonnet, and her muslin frock, which had started the day crisp and fresh, hanging limply about her. It had been a very trying morning, and to meet Monsieur Roland when she knew she was far from looking her best was almost the last straw.

He was sitting on a table-tomb beside the path, reading something on a sheet of paper, but as she approached, he stood up, folded the paper and put it in his pocket, and removed his broad-brimmed demi-bateau, waiting for her to come level with him.

'Good day, Miss Calvert,' he said, his English only very slightly accented. He looked particularly clean and tidy, as he always did, and Lucinda wondered how he always managed to look so spruce on what must be a very small income. He taught French to a group of the children of some of the professional people in the town, but the fees paid by the parents could not possibly be enough for him to live on, yet his dark clothes never looked shabby or mended, and his linen always appeared unfrayed and undarned. She supposed that he must have some other source of income, and assumed it was some sort of writing, for he was often to be seen with a notebook and pencil. There was certainly no other possibility that she could think of, for he was an *émigré* who had escaped from France during the Reign of Terror with little more than a change of clothes.

He was handsome, in a dark and melancholy fashion, broad-shouldered and well-set-up, with black hair touched with grey at the temples, an aquiline nose, deep-set, very dark eyes, and a charming smile which lit up his face as he spoke to her.

'Good day, Monsieur Roland,' she replied, stopping to return his smile. 'It's very warm again.'

'Indeed. You 'ave been visiting your poor folk again? I 'ope that there are none injured from last night's explosion?' (He had trouble with his aspirates.)

'No one was hurt,' Lucinda assured him. 'Father sent to enquire, and it appears they were only testing powder.'

'Good! I'm much relieved to 'ear it. Was it the new invention that they try out?'

'I've no idea,' Lucinda replied. 'I think it was just a quality test. What makes you think it might be something new?'

He shrugged. 'I meant Colonel Congreve's invention—I still think of them as something new. 'Ave you 'eard 'ow they progress?'

'The rockets, you mean? I've not heard anything about them since they were used against Boulogne last year. It's not the sort of thing that even Colonel Congreve would discuss with a lady!' Lucinda replied, laughing. 'You must ask Colonel Long, though I don't think he's very interested, being an infantry officer— they seem to have no time for artillery!'

'Then 'e should be interested!' Monsieur Roland said seriously. 'Much can be done with artillery, and it may be that this new invention may 'elp to defeat Bonaparte!'

'I'm sure he will be defeated before long, and you'll be able to go home at last.' Lucinda tried to sound comforting and hopeful, but in her heart she feared it would take many more years, and more than William Congreve's somewhat erratic rockets, to bring an end to the war. She did, in fact, know a little about the weapon, for Colonel Congreve was given to talking enthusiastically about whatever topic held his attention at the moment to anyone who would listen, and she had met him two or three times at the Longs'.

'Yes. I mustn't lose 'ope.' Monsieur Roland sounded very melancholy, but then he brightened and said, 'But your mother's 'as very kindly invited me to dine on

Tuesday, to meet the new sensation of Wood'am.'

'Oh.' For a moment Lucinda looked as disconcerted as she felt, for she knew nothing of a projected dinner-party, and wondered if Cook had yet been informed, with strawberries, gooseberries, mulberries and cherries all falling from their bushes and trees faster than she could transform them into jam and preserves. 'Yes, of course,' she continued. 'I'm sure you'll enjoy meeting Mr Harris—he's lived abroad a great deal. I must hurry, Monsieur Roland. I'm sorry, but I shall be late for luncheon.'

James and John, after a preliminary whirring, ting-tanged to confirm her words, a dozen sonorous booms from Gabriel drowned whatever reply Monsieur Roland made as he bowed in farewell, and Lucinda hurried down the path, running full tilt into Mr Harris as she rounded the corner of the church.

'Ah, Miss Lucinda!' he exclaimed, catching her by the shoulders to steady her. 'I've returned your shawl. I was sorry to miss seeing you, but your father said you were about your good works.'

Lucinda was taken completely unawares by the sudden encounter, and even more so by the extraordinary sensation which started in her shoulders, where his hands were gripping her, and spread through her body like a warm shiver. To add to her discomfiture, he sounded ironic to the point of sarcasm, and her reaction to the multiple surprise was a flash of anger at the note of mockery which she detected in his words.

'Someone has to try to help the poor and the old!' she replied sharply, stepping back out of his grasp. 'The Poor Law Guardians can do little enough for them!'

'True,' he replied, 'but are there no maiden ladies of middle age with nothing to occupy their idle hours?

Young ladies should be enjoying themselves, not risking their health in sick-visiting!'

Lucinda was suddenly very conscious of the sight she must present, and turned her face away to wipe a trickle of sweat from the side of her nose with the back of her hand, unaware that, in doing so, she rubbed a smudge of soot across her cheek in a long streak.

The large carriage-dog which she had seen trotting beside Mr Harris's mare on an earlier occasion suddenly appeared from behind a gravestone which he had been investigating, and came over to sniff dubiously at Lucinda's skirts. He was a fine animal, gleaming white between his black spots, and Lucinda exclaimed, 'What a beautiful dog! Is he yours?'

'Yes. He's quite docile—no need to be nervous of him.' Mr Harris smiled to himself as he realised that his words were unnecessary, for Lucinda had bent down to address the dog directly and fondle his ears, telling him he was a very handsome fellow. 'His name is Arthur.'

'After King Arthur?' Lucinda enquired, letting the dog lick her hand.

'No—after Sir Arthur Wellesley, in fact. He gave me the dog as a pup.'

'You know Sir Arthur?' She looked up, startled. 'He was often here when he was commanding the defence forces against invasion. Colonel Long says he's the only man he knows who could outmatch Bonaparte!'

'Yes, I dare say he will, if he ever gets the chance!' Mr Harris sounded amused. 'Unfortunately, the War Office thinks he can only fight Indians, and he's less popular with his superiors than he is with the ladies! But we're keeping you, I fear, and your Mama was wondering some time ago whether you would return in time for luncheon.'

'Oh dear!' Lucinda gave him a rueful little smile,

wondering if her mother had gone on at great length about her lateness, for she had a habit of making the most of any complaint. 'I'd better hurry, then. Thank you for bringing my shawl.'

Mr Harris touched his hat-brim in salute, smiled in his enigmatic fashion, and went on his way, Arthur at his heel, leaving Lucinda, hastening through the Rectory side-gate and across the garden, with a nasty suspicion that he might have thought that she had left the shawl behind on purpose.

Her parents were already sat down to luncheon when she joined them, pausing only to wash her face and hands and tidy herself before entering the dining-room. Her mother greeted her with 'Really, Lucinda, one would think that, with those dreadful bells clanging the hour fit to wake the dead, you could at least manage to be on time! I despair of you, I really do! It was sensible to have the foresight to leave your shawl last night, but downright inept to be from home when Mr Harris brought it back.'

'I didn't leave it a'purpose, Mama!' Lucinda protested, and her father said quietly, 'I'm glad to hear it.'

But his comment passed unnoticed by his wife, who was too busy exclaiming, 'I might have known it, of course!' She raised her eyes to heaven and pushed away her plate, her disappointment in her daughter clearly having robbed her of her uncertain appetite. 'Mr Calvert, what is to become of your daughter? Nigh on twenty, and with no more idea of how to catch a husband than she has of flying!'

'I think Lucy has no need to lay traps for a husband,' the Rector replied with quiet authority. 'And I beg you'll not speak of marriage on those terms! Marriages are made in heaven, Mrs Calvert, and the Lord will send

Lucy a husband if and when He thinks fit.'

For one dreadful moment Lucinda thought her mother might be about to say something slighting concerning the Lord's tardiness, for she certainly opened her mouth as if to do so, but then remembered her position in life, closed her lips tightly and made a curious sound between a snort and a sigh.

After a discreet interval, during which she ate rabbit pie and vegetables which had grown cold and unappetising through her lateness, Lucinda ventured, 'I met Monsieur Roland in the churchyard. He said you'd invited him to dine on Tuesday.'

'Yes. There are so few cultured gentlemen in such a small town whom one would consider worthy of the notice of a travelled person.' Mrs Calvert drew her plate back to its place and essayed a little more of her luncheon, no doubt encouraged by her own thoughtfulness. 'There are the Longs, of course, with whom Mr Harris is already well acquainted. It appears that he was at Cambridge with the Colonel's younger brother—the one who was so sadly lost the year before last at Trafalgar. I shall not ask the Martins this time, for Miss Martin does tend to put herself forward a little, and this room is too small for more than ten to sit down to dinner in any degree of comfort.'

'Ten!' exclaimed Lucinda, ignoring the slight cast upon her friend. 'But, Mama, you've only mentioned four guests so far.'

'Seven, with ourselves,' Mrs Calvert replied. 'There will be Mr Jones, who is also a university man and can make himself quite agreeable in exchange for a good dinner, poor man, and Mrs Willoughby, whose late husband was in India with the Company' (she meant the East India Company) 'and Miss Enston.'

'Miss Enston!' Lucinda was so surprised that she

forgot to mention that Mr Harris had implied that he had no connection with India.

'Certainly!' Mrs Calvert allowed herself a little smile of satisfaction at her own Machiavellian planning. 'She's a worthy little soul, and it might be quite useful to have it widely known that Mr Harris is on terms of close friendship with the Rectory.'

'I've always thought it advisable,' Mr Calvert observed in a detached manner, 'to know something of a man's background before one admits him to terms of close friendship.'

'So cautious, Mr Calvert!' his wife rallied him. 'And how many beggars and worse have taken you in with their sad tales? I vow I've a better ability to judge character than you, any day, and my intuition tells me that Mr Harris is a gentleman of the highest character.'

As there was no reply to that which might safely be voiced by a husband or a daughter, luncheon proceeded in silence for a few minutes while Annie removed the dishes and brought in a bowl of gooseberry fool. When she had withdrawn, Lucinda said cautiously, 'Is Cook aware that there will be ten for dinner on Tuesday?'

Her mother gave her a pitying glance. 'My dear child! Give me credit for having my wits! Do you imagine that I'm not aware of the continual smell of jam about the place, or the fact that we seem to be living on gooseberries and strawberries? I've told Cook that she may call in her two sisters to help on both Monday and Tuesday, and Mrs Howe, the washing-woman, may come on Tuesday to help with the washing-up. It's well worth the expense of a few shillings to see that all goes well and Cook is not Put Out!'

'Mrs Howe will be glad of the extra money, with Duke not able to work,' observed the Rector.

'Duke not working?' Mrs Calvert asked. 'Why ever

not? He's quite the most useful handyman in the town, and I'd have thought he'd never want for work.'

'He was mending the Coggets' roof last week, and their ladder broke,' Lucinda said grimly, for she blamed Mr Cogget for not seeing that his ladder was in proper repair. 'Poor Duke broke a bone in his ankle and is laid up, and Mr Coggett says it was his own fault.'

'In that case,' said her mother, who was as kind and practical as anyone when she forgot that she was an invalid with an unmarried daughter, 'Mrs Howe shall come on Monday as well. She's a good hand with pastry. I'll see what else I can find for her to do until Marmaduke is working again. There's a pair of sheets to sides-to-middle, for one thing.'

After luncheon, Lucinda changed into a fresh muslin, put on her bonnet, collected a lidded basket from the scullery, and went to call on Mrs Smith, the landlady of the Black Swan. The inn was in West Street, a few doors along from the Rectory, past the pin-mill, and it was necessary to cross the mill-stream by means of a wooden bridge to get to it.

The bridge was narrow, for it was used only by people on foot, horses and vehicles crossing by means of the shallow ford below the bridge. Lucinda paused in the middle and leaned on the handrail to look down into the water. She could hear the wheel clacking in the mill behind her, so she knew that the sluice was open, but there was not very much water coming through, and she wondered how long it would be before a deputation of farmers and mill-owners waited on her father to request prayers for rain.

When she went on her way, she was not surprised to find that she had been joined by Fred, who stalked majestically just in front of her in a semi-detached fashion, for the cat had a long-standing relationship with the Black Swan's tabby queen, and it was one of the offspring of this feline marriage which was the object of Lucinda's visit.

The kitten—or, rather, young cat—was now eight months old, but had not been taken by a would-be provider of a home for a cat of mousing ancestry simply because she was a female, but Lucinda knew that she had inherited her father's abilities in that direction, for she had caught her first mouse when she was not much bigger than a mouse herself. She was a handsome creature, with her father's colouring and dictatorial manner.

The matter was arranged with Mrs Smith in a very short time, and Lucinda left the landlady's parlour with Fred's daughter mewing in a puzzled manner inside the lidded basket, and called at the Swan's stables in the hope that Mr Harris's groom, or at least his horse, might still be there. The ostler, however, told her that the gentleman had left more than an hour ago, so there was no help for it but to set off on the long walk to Pinnacles.

Her way lay along East Street to the edge of the town, and then across the fields, keeping close to the hedges for what shade she could find from the hot sun, carefully surveying each pasture field before she entered it to see what beasts it might contain, and equally carefully shutting the gates behind her, and keeping well to the edge of the cornfields, which were now almost ready for harvest.

It was very quiet. Most of the labourers were working in the meadows down by the river, bringing in the last of the hay. A few birds were singing in the trees, and some swallows swooped high up in the cloudless sky, while, higher still, the disembodied voice of a lark twittered and trilled. Lucinda put down the basket to rest for a moment, and shaded her eyes with her hands as she looked up and tried to see the little bird, but it was too high.

The cat had settled down in the basket and was quiet, so Lucinda peeped in to see if she was all right. A pair of large, impersonal green eyes looked through her as she did so, and then a tail-tip twitched indifferently across the nose, and the eyes closed as the cat went back to sleep.

As Lucinda reached the beginning of the rise up to the Forest, she began to wish that Mr Harris had not expressed such an urgent need for a cat. She sat down to rest for a while under an oak, where there was a convenient log. It had been there for as long as she could remember and she had often rested on it on her way to Cob End, but she wondered now how much longer it would remain, for she was now on Pinnacles land, and no doubt Mr Harris would have it removed if he meant to put these fields to the plough.

It was pleasant in the shade. A trickle of water ran in the ditch behind her, the flow from a spring further up in the Forest. Crickets were fiddling in the grass, butterflies were sunning themselves on the blue scabious, and there was a drowsy humming of bees amid the buttercups and orchis. She lifted the lid of the basket and enquired again if the cat was all right, and was rewarded with a rumbling purr.

'You should have a good home with Mr Harris,' she informed the animal. 'Your father took a liking to him and gave him a mouse, and he seems fond of animals, but he has a dog. You won't mind that, though, for you're used to them, aren't you?' (Mr Smith of the Black Swan bred lurchers.)

The cat made no audible reply, so Lucinda abandoned the one-sided conversation and fell to thinking, wondering to whom Amy had been referring in her mysterious talk of someone who took no notice of her. It was difficult to imagine anyone not taking notice of Amy, for if she was not precisely beautiful, she was lively and attractive.

Perhaps it was Monsieur Roland. He was a serious-minded man, but he had little in his life to make him otherwise, poor man! Lucinda tried to imagine what it must be like to be a poor exile in a country at war with one's own, and was thankful, not for the first time, that she had been born English, and did not have to leave England for any reason, good or bad.

Mr Harris had lived abroad—a great deal, he had said—and had dreamed of settling down in the English countryside, but perhaps he would find Woodham dull, and Woodham people boring, with their narrow parochial interests. Why, she had only ever been to London once, and that was a mere twenty miles away!

In the distance, she heard Gabriel's voice reminding her that the afternoon was slipping away, so she picked up the basket and went on up the hill, leaving her usual route towards Cob End, and striking across to join the Pinnacles drive.

When she reached it, she glanced along to her right, and saw that there were men at work amid the piles of bricks by the lodge. They seemed to be building a large wooden hut of some sort, which she supposed they would use as a shelter for themselves and their tools while they were working on whatever Mr Harris was having built.

As she crossed the last field before the archway into the gardens, the donkeys came to investigate her, and she stroked their soft noses and admired their plump sides, for they were in excellent condition. One made a determined effort to steal her bonnet with a view to eating it, but she was acquainted with the taking ways of the species and escaped unscathed, going on to the arch, pausing in its shade to wipe her hands and face with her handkerchief, shake the burrs and grass-seeds from her skirts, and set her bonnet straight, and then marched in good order to the front door and pulled the bell.

A footman answered the door, and said in a distant, formal tone, 'Good afternoon, Miss Calvert.'

'Is Mr Harris at home?' she asked, refusing to be made nervous by a servant, however superciliously he might look upon a person who arrived alone and on foot.

'I will enquire. Pray be pleased to come in.'

Lucinda entered the hall, which was, in fact, a well-furnished room, and sat down on a small sofa with her basket at her feet, while the footman vanished into the interior of the house. It was very quiet and cool, and there was a pleasant smell of flowers and beeswax.

Rapid footsteps roused her from the somewhat torpid state into which she had lapsed, and Mr Harris came hurrying into the hall, the footman following at a more dignified pace.

'My dear Miss Calvert, how pleasant to see you! George—tea, if you please. On the terrace, I think.'

Lucinda picked up her basket, which Mr Harris at once took from her, but it lurched sharply as he did so and an indignant remark from inside it intimated that the cat's first meeting with her prospective new host was not. starting very auspiciously.

'It's the cat,' said Lucinda.

'Indeed, so it sounded!' Mr Harris exclaimed. He put the basket on a convenient table, opened the lid and lifted out the ruffled feline.

'Well, my beauty,' he said, settling her into the crook of his arm and rubbing her soothingly behind the ears. 'You're the image of your old dad, I do declare. I trust you're as talented. Is this the queen you mentioned last night?'

The question was addressed to Lucinda, who replied,

'Yes. She's Fred's daughter by the tabby at the Black Swan—a good mousing strain on both sides. She's eight months, and hasn't been found a home because most people don't want the bother of frequent kittens.'

'Quite so. She'll do very well here, though, for there's not another cat nearer than the town, as far as I know. If I'm wrong, there's no matter, for there's always room for a few more cats in the stables. Has she a name?'

'Mrs Smith at the Swan called her Tiddles,' Lucinda said apologetically.

'Tiddles!' Mr Harris was clearly disgusted. 'A lady of breeding and handsome appearance should have a concomitant name . . . Would you care for Charlotte, madam?'

This was addressed to the cat, who purred and closed her eyes ecstatically, but because she liked being rubbed behind the ears, not because the name meant anything to her.

George the footman had not left the hall when the erstwhile Tiddles first made her presence known, and the sound had made him turn to see what was afoot. He had remained, looking at the cat with interest from a distance. Mr Harris looked up and saw him.

'Ah, George!' he said. 'This is Charlotte. Would you be so kind as to take her to the kitchen and introduce her to everyone, particularly the mice? I think you are quite fond of animals?'

'Yes, sir!' George's formal mode of speech left him in his enthusiasm over the cat, which he had taken into a close embrace. 'Specially cats. I love cats!'

'Then you shall have charge of Charlotte. She may have the run of the house, but try to keep her out of the kitchen gardens, unless the gardeners think there may be work for her there. Oh, and keep her in at night, for fear of foxes.'

Footman and cat departed, and Mr Harris thought to call, 'And don't forget the tea!' after them, then conducted Lucinda through the house to the terrace, where a table and some comfortably cushioned chairs were standing in the shade of a copper beech. A number of sheets of paper, held down by a small, thick book, lay on the table, and appeared to be covered by rows of letters, written in pencil, with many of the letters crossed out.

Lucinda stood by the table for a few seconds, looking down at them, while Mr Harris placed a chair more in the shade for her, and plumped up the cushions. Then he turned to invite her to sit down, and saw what she was looking at.

'A little idle scribbling,' he said a shade too quickly to be natural. 'Pray sit down, Miss Calvert.' He gathered the papers up hastily and put them under the cushion of the seat of another chair, then sat down on it, giving Lucinda what she felt to be a calculating look as he did so. She was a little embarrassed as she assumed that he thought she had been overly curious about his papers, and she supposed that they were something personal— poetry, perhaps—but she was too well bred to have looked at them properly. There was a slightly awkward pause, as she did not know what to say.

'I trust that your horse is being attended to?' he said suddenly. 'Did you ride or drive?'

'I walked,' she replied, surprised.

'Walked, my dear girl? On such a hot day?' Mr Harris seemed quite shocked, so Lucinda, surprised at being called his 'dear girl', hastened to add, 'It's not far across the fields—the road curves quite a lot to ease the gradient, you see, but the paths run fairly straight up the hill.'

There was another pause, during which Mr Harris looked at her quizzically and said nothing. She found herself continuing, 'We don't really have a coachman, and only two horses. Father puts one to the gig when he goes about, and drives himself, and the stable-lad is also the gardener. The other horse isn't broken to riding . . .' She suddenly thought what a lot of confused nonsense she had been uttering.

'And, pray, what is the coachman in real life? A white rat with pink eyes, or perhaps the curate . . .?' Mr Harris enquired solemnly, his grey eyes looking quite warm and genuinely amused.

Lucinda suddenly felt much more at ease with him, and replied equally solemnly, 'No, the sexton!' and they both laughed.

George and another footman appeared with the tea-tray and a selection of dainty cakes, and George, at his most wooden and formal, murmured, 'You may care to know, sir, that Charlotte has killed three mice and consumed a plate of beef and a saucer of milk. It appears that she does not eat the mice.'

'Excellent!' exclaimed Mr Harris. 'Not ten minutes in the house, and already had her paws under the table! Thank you.'

The footmen withdrew, and Mr Harris invited Lucinda to take charge of the tea-pouring, which she did a trifle nervously, for the porcelain cups and dishes looked remarkably delicate. There were no mishaps, however, and she sipped her tea gratefully, enjoying the rest and the cool shade, listening to the gentle sounds of the garden—bees, a contented chucking from a drowsy bird, and doves cooing somewhere round the corner of the house. The only flaw in her enjoyment was a consciousness of the presence of Mr Harris, which was oddly disturbing. He did not seem to expect her to make conversation, but lounged comfortably in his chair, drinking his tea and contemplating his rose-bushes through half-closed eyes, yet every fibre of her body seemed to be aware of him. Her thoughts, which normally followed a reasonably coherent pattern, seemed to flit about like an agitated moth, wondering where he had come from, what he did before he came here, what those rows of letters on his papers signified, whether he thought she had left her shawl here on purpose . . .

'It seems a pity to spoil so perfect a silence by sordid considerations of commerce,' he said suddenly, 'but how much do I owe you?'

She started and looked at him blankly for a moment, then collected her wits and replied, 'Nothing—Mrs Smith was pleased to find her a good home.'

'I'll offer her something when I next put up my horse there, then.' Mr Harris stretched out his legs and visibly relaxed still more. 'A couple of brace of rabbits, perhaps . . . Your mother very kindly invited me to dine on Tuesday.'

'Yes.' Lucinda meant to say more, but seemed to have lost her tongue, for nothing further emerged.

'I had meant to ask the Rector when I called this morning, but I forgot.' Mr Harris went on, after another pause, 'Perhaps you can tell me—what is the arrangement about pews?'

'Pews?' Lucinda said blankly.

'In the church. Are they rented?'

'Oh—yes. Well, the gentry usually rent, but the majority are free. There is a Pinnacles pew—or at least it was always held by the Hooks, and has stood empty since—well, since Sir Robert was killed. The People's Warden arranges about the rents, if you wish.'

'And the People's Warden is . . . ?' Mr Harris was contemplating the toe of his boot, so Lucinda took the opportunity to study his face, replying 'Mr Morris,' as she did so. His nose was straight and strong, and there was always a suggestion of a smile about his mouth, and a purposeful look about his chin. 'He's the landlord of the Wyvern in the market square,' she added, 'and Mr Martin is the Rector's Warden.'

'And there is a service every Sunday?'

'Yes. Mattins at ten in the morning, and Evensong at three, for the servants and labourers.'

'I've known places where the incumbent took servive only once a month,' Mr Harris commented.

Lucinda put down her cup and asked Mr Harris if she might refill his, but he replied, 'No, thank you. Do you take another, and some of those cakes, or there'll be revolution in the kitchen if they go back untouched! I mean to cut you a few roses. They're old bushes, but they've been trimmed up well and are bearing some fine blooms.'

He got to his feet, felt in his pockets, and produced a folding knife of ungentlemanly size, took her basket, and went down the steps to the second terrace, where most of the roses grew. Lucinda drank another cup of tea and ate two or three cakes, watching him moving about among the bushes. After a while, he stopped cutting roses and came back up the steps just as Lucinda, putting her cup and dish down on the table, moved the tray a little, not seeing that a book which he had been using as a paperweight was lying on the far side of it. The book fell to the ground and Lucinda dived to pick it up in some confusion, and, naturally, looked at the spine to see if it had been damaged. She had only time to see the words *Des Codes et Chiffres* before Mr Harris took it from her, saying, 'Thank you. Careless of me to leave it there.'

'I hope it may not be damaged!' Lucinda said, trying to see if the corners had been bent.

'Not at all,' he replied firmly, but not looking at it. 'See, here are a few roses for you to take home.'

'How kind!' Lucinda exclaimed, for the basket

seemed to be full of fat buds, pink, white, red, and even some white ones splashed and striped with red, and all most delightfully scented. 'Mama will be delighted—she loves roses!'

'They are for you,' Mr Harris said. 'Unless you have an aversion to them?'

'No, of course not!' she exclaimed. 'Thank you very much for them, and for the tea. I—I should be going now, I think.'

'Pray sit down again for a few minutes, Miss Calvert. I'll order my carriage. It's far too hot for you to walk all that way home.'

'Oh, but . . .' Lucinda protested, but not with much vehemence.

'The cattle don't get enough exercise. Excuse me.' Mr Harris went into the house, taking the book with him, and presently returned without it. 'Shall we stroll gently round to the front? The carriage should be ready for you by the time we get there.'

It took only a quarter of an hour to drive down to the Rectory, and Lucinda enjoyed riding in Mr Harris's spanking new carriage with the hoods down and a groom on the box beside the driver, behind a fine matched pair of greys. She passed Miss Enston along East Street, and could not resist waving to her, then looked back to see the lady rush into Mrs Harvey's house to tell what she had just seen, which made Lucinda smile to herself as she waved regally to Monsieur Roland in the market square.

Outside the church, the driver drew into the kerb, the groom got down to open the door and let down the steps, and Lucinda was handed down in fine style. She thanked the driver and groom, who both saluted, and patted the horses before going sedately towards the Rectory side-gate.

Mr Jones was just coming out, and he stood aside, raising his hat and twinkling his blue eyes at her. 'There's glory, now!' he said in a remarkably good Welsh accent for one who claimed no recent Celtic ancestry. 'Mr Harris's carriage, is it? His man handles the ribbons well!'

Lucinda turned to look, and saw that the coachman had turned horses and carriage in one smooth circling movement in the limited area between the churchyard wall and the ford.

'I'd love to be able to drive a pair of horses'—Mr Jones said dreamily—'in a high-perch phaeton. It must be grand to be rich and powerful!'

Lucinda looked at him in surprise. 'Why, I thought you enjoyed your work!'

'I do. It's what I was born for, but I see so much need and poverty, even here in Woodham, and with more money and important contacts, I could do so much more! I could marry my ideal helpmeet . . .'

His voice faded away suddenly, and Lucinda, glancing at him, saw that he was looking wistful and melancholy. She suspected that he was following his own thoughts and had forgotten about her. 'Have you found her, then?' she asked gently.

Mr Jones started, and gave her an odd, rather hunted, look. 'A man may set his heart on the stars, but usually he must learn to be content with a penny candle,' he said wryly, 'and be thankful if he can afford one! Good afternoon, Miss Calvert.'

'Good afternoon, Mr Jones.'

Lucinda went into the garden and found her mother reclining on a wicker sofa which hung from a stout branch of the walnut tree and had a canvas canopy suspended above it. With plenty of cushions, it could be very comfortable, swinging gently in the shade, but Mrs

Calvert rarely used it, for it took an exceptionally hot day to persuade her to sit out of doors.

'Why, whatever have you there?' she asked, catching sight of Lucinda's basket.

'Mr Harris gave me some roses. He wanted a cat, so I took him Mrs Smith's last kitten, and he filled my basket with roses in exchange.'

'You've not walked all that way up there and back in this heat!' Mrs Calvert cried in alarm. 'Why, it's enough to bring on a megrim, and you'll be *sun-burned*, with only that shallow-brimmed bonnet.'

'Mr Harris sent me home in his carriage,' Lucinda replied soothingly, 'and I kept to the shade of the hedgerows walking up there. Besides, Mama, I don't burn.'

'But the slightest browning from the sun is most unbecoming,' Mrs Calvert insisted. 'I won't have you looking like a farm-wench! Go to the still-room at once, and find some of that whitening lotion—the one which Mrs Martin recommended. You must mix it with fresh lemon-juice . . .'

'But, Mama, we have no lemons!' Lucinda protested.

'Then send Annie out to buy one, at once!' Mrs Calvert commanded with the vigour and adamantine purpose which she could summon up the strength to employ only in the most dire emergencies. 'Really, Lucinda, I despair of you! Have you no sense of what are the most important things in life?'

CHAPTER FOUR

MRS CALVERT usually attended Mattins, although sometimes in a somewhat martyred fashion, but the hot weather, which had lasted too long for most people's liking, had become, she said, too much for her, and she decided to stay in her sitting-room, despite the Rector's mild protest that the interior of the church was the coolest place in the town.

Lucinda found that he was quite right when she entered the great building, for the thick stone Norman walls retained the usual chill atmosphere, and she was glad of her shawl as she walked slowly up the nave, smiling and nodding to various acquaintances. She did not speak, of course, for church-going was a serious business in those days, and only necessary words were spoken, and those in a whisper unless they formed part of the service.

The Rectory pew was in the chancel, facing crossways, and from it Lucinda had a good view of the body of the church and of the congregation which almost filled it. After she had prayed for a few minutes and found the right places in her Prayer Book, she discreetly looked about her, first admiring, as she always did, the great grooved pillars and the strong chevron-decorated arches which rose in three tiers—nave arcade, triforium and clerestory—to a disappointingly plain wooden ceiling.

The morning sun was pouring in through the windows, most of which contained clear glass, and the stone shone pale gold, almost the colour of wheat-straw.

Most of the congregation had arrived, for the Rector could be quite sharp with latecomers, and an unusual stirring in their ranks caught Lucinda's attention. At first she could see nothing out of the ordinary. Mr and Mrs Martin and Amy were just taking their seats in the front pew, which was marked by the churchwarden's crowned staff in its holder by the central aisle, but even they were not keeping their eyes down in a seemly fashion, but looking across to the front pew on the other side, which had not been occupied for years.

It was occupied now, and it was that which had caused the stir. Mr Harris was calmly sitting down in it, dropping his gloves into his upturned beaver hat on the seat beside him. He then sank to his knees, bent his head for a few moments, then sat down again and looked about him, but, Lucinda thought, at the building, not the people. She felt a lifting of her spirits, which she assumed was due to seeing the Pinnacles pew occupied again after so many years.

The bells, which had been ringing merrily, stopped suddenly, and one—Raphael, she thought—took up the slow strokes of the five minute bell, warning the sluggards that they were about to earn a rectorial reprimand, and, incidentally, giving the ringers time to come down and take their seats. Mr Calvert had made it plain that he did not care for the custom of the ringers retiring to the nearest inn during the service.

There was the usual scramble of last-minute arrivals, and then the little band of fiddlers and the sole cellist struck up the first hymn, the congregation rose, and they began to sing in a ragged fashion, gaining confidence as they advanced into the first verse. The Rector and Mr

Jones came side by side up the aisle, and the service began.

It was the Rector's turn to officiate, so Mr Jones retired to his desk, which was almost opposite Lucinda's place across the chancel, and he sat down in an oddly uncomfortable-looking position, half-turned towards the congregation, which Lucinda thought unusual, for he normally sat very straight and kept his eyes on his service book. She glanced across at him from time to time, and found that, whether he was sitting or standing, his face was always half-turned to his right—the only time it was not was during the prayers—and she came to the conclusion that he was watching someone.

She also noticed that Mr Harris seemed well acquainted with the complications of the Prayer Book and found his way about without difficulty, and he preserved a suitable air of grave dignity, except that, when the Rector published the banns of marriage between 'William Henry Plomer and Jennifer Briggs, both of this parish', he looked quite deliberately across at Lucinda and grinned broadly.

The Rector was not an inspired preacher. In fact, he had half a dozen fat books in which he had written down some two hundred carefully composed sermons when he was first ordained, and he worked his way through them on ordinary Sundays, only writing a new one for the Great Festivals, and if the Bishop came. Lucinda had heard most of them several times, for he liked to rehearse the more difficult ones over to her on the previous evening, and she tended to allow her attention to wander as soon as her father climbed into the pulpit and uttered his first 'My friends . . .'

On this occasion the Pinnacles pew seemed to be acting as a magnet, and, if she was not careful, her eyes constantly returned to it. During the sermon, she had to make a conscious effort to look discreetly about the rest of the building, moving her head as little as possible, to note who was missing from his or her usual place, who had a new bonnet, whose children were fidgeting, who had gone to sleep—all the little things which either her father or her mother would wish to know after the service.

Lucinda then happened to note, for her own interest, that Mr Jones was sitting straight, with his head bowed as though in private prayer. Almost immediately after, she saw that Amy Martin was now sitting with her head turned unnaturally, neither towards the pulpit nor straight ahead but somewhere between the two, and the two pieces of information seemed to fit together. Surely, before, Mr Jones had been looking at Amy, and now Amy was looking at Mr Jones. Lucinda stored the thought away for consideration at a more suitable time.

After the service, the congregation left the church in a quiet and seemly fashion, and erupted into a chatter outside. Mr Calvert and Mr Jones stood side by side in the shade of the porch to exchange a few words with everyone who passed, the players in the gallery held an impromptu concert as they practised the hymns for Evensong, and the altar-servers scurried about their duties. Lucinda collected from the vestry an altar-cloth which needed mending and stopped for a word with Mr Gibbs, who combined vergering with his sexton's duties.

By the time she walked out into the brightness of the mid-day sun, almost everyone had gone, for the heat struck with considerable strength after the cool stillness inside the church. Only the swifts were wheeling and screaming high above the gilded cock on the tower, and Mr Harris stood talking to Mr Jones, his dog close to heel, just inside the porch.

'Good morning, Miss Calvert,' he said as Lucinda emerged from the inner door.

'Good morning, Mr Harris. You didn't leave poor Arthur out in the sun, I trust?'

'No, he sat in the porch and minded the fire-engine, like a sensible dog.' He gestured towards the town's fire-pump, which was kept in the porch. 'I've been making the acquaintance of Mr Jones, who has the right attitude to dogs, despite having been at the wrong university!'

'Were you at Oxford?' Lucinda asked the Curate, never having thought to enquire before.

'Yes. At Jesus.'

Mr Harris laughed. 'I should have guessed! It's said that, if one stands in the quad at Jesus and shouts "Mr Jones!", half the windows in the college will open, and the inmates reply, "What is it?"' He said the last three words with a Welsh intonation, which amused Mr Jones.

'True enough!' he admitted.

'How is Charlotte?' Lucinda enquired, stroking the head of Arthur, who had come to sit beside her.

'The tally up to this morning was thirty-seven mice and two rats, but she's slowing down now, mainly from a shortage of rodents, I believe. Rumour reports that parties of *émigré* mice have been seen fleeing across the garden with their belongings piled on hand-carts, or carried in bundles on their backs, and the rat War Council is considering whether to fight a last-ditch stand in the stables or make a strategic withdrawal to the Forest. Pray tell Fred that his daughter does him credit!'

'All his children do him credit,' Mr Jones volunteered, 'apart from one young scamp who killed my second-best wig!'

'You must find a wig intolerably hot in this weather!' observed Mr Harris, looking at the old-fashioned Parsonical Bob which Mr Jones was wearing, as all clergy-men were expected to do.

'I wear it only in church,' he replied, taking it off and twirling it on one finger.

'The powder must be a nuisance on your cassock?'

Mr Jones tapped the side of his nose with his finger in a quizzical fashion, and confided in a low voice. 'White horsehair, sir. No powder! Ah, which reminds me, Miss Calvert—your mother sent Annie to say that she wishes you to return home speedily.'

Lucinda experienced a curious sinking in her spirits such as she had not felt since those occasions in her childhood when she had been summoned to leave a party, or finish a game which she had been particularly enjoying, in order to do something less appealing. She bade the gentlemen good day and hastened back to the Rectory. As she had half-expected, it was not for any important or urgent reason that she had been sent for, but only for a discussion about her wardrobe.

Mrs Calvert had spent some part of the morning looking at her daughter's small collection of frocks and gowns, and had come to the conclusion that she needed some new ones. 'You have only two evening gowns!' she exclaimed as soon as Lucinda walked into her bedroom and found her sitting on the bed with cottons, silks and muslins strewn around her. 'You wore the green on Thursday, and the yellow is shabby. In any case, the colour doesn't suit you in the least, and I can't imagine why you chose it!'

Lucinda refrained from replying that, in fact, her mother had chosen the yellow, and merely said, 'I fear there's no time to make a new one before Tuesday, even if we sat up all night stitching. I thought I would take the ribbons off on the green, and put on some different ones, and perhaps some lace round the neck . . .'

'Perhaps we could go to London tomorrow and buy something,' Mrs Calvert mused aloud.

'London!' exclaimed Lucinda. 'Now, Mama, you know that Father is to dine with the Bishop tomorrow and will need the carriage, and I'm certain that you'd not wish to drive twenty miles into London in the gig, with either you or me driving! I'll put silver ribbons on the green, and perhaps you might lend me your silver lace collar.'

In the event, the green gown looked quite different with its silver trimming, and Mrs Calvert gave it grudging approval when, having finished the alterations hurriedly at the last moment, Lucinda went downstairs in it on Tuesday evening, the last of the silver ribbon threaded through her ringlets.

As might have been expected, Miss Enston was the first to arrive, a plump little lady of uncertain age, who was always so eager to be at the point where something was happening that she permanently leaned forward from the hips, so that her head might be a foot in front of the rest of her, in order to allow her eyes and ears the advantage of early arrival. She had bright little brown eyes and a sharp nose which was given to twitching at its end, and Lucinda sometimes wondered if Fred was ever tempted to pounce on her, for she looked very much like a mouse in a poplin gown and a lace cap with old-fashioned lappets.

'I am so looking forward to this evening!' she announced as she shed her bonnet and shawl and entered the parlour. 'Such excitement, to meet a new neighbour, especially one who has been to such interesting places! I believe Jamaica is quite paradisical, except for those dreadful hurricanes, and one has read so much about the majesty and grandeur of the Austrian court!'

'How is it,' Mrs Calvert enquired *sotto voce* of her

daughter—Miss Enston having cornered the Rector to demand an explanation of some obscure point in his sermon of the Sunday before last—'that she manages to know everyone's business, and to the best of my knowledge she's not even spoken to the man yet!'

'I think she reads minds,' Lucinda replied, not altogether seriously. At that moment, Annie answered the door bell and admitted Mr Harris. The parlour door was open, and Lucinda could see him in the hall, but she heard his voice first, and was dismayed by the flutter it caused in the pit of her stomach, and the sudden warmth in her cheeks, which made her a little distracted in her greeting. Matters were not improved by the quizzical look he gave her as he bent to kiss her proffered hand, or by her consciousness of Miss Enston's sharp eyes in the background.

When all the guests were assembled, the parlour was quite crowded, and Mrs Calvert, in good looks with the excitement of her party, and forgetting her poor health, made a bold decision and desired the Rector to open the glazed doors into the garden, which were normally kept fast shut, with a screen before them for fear of a draught. Mr Calvert found them difficult to move, the hinges being quite rusty, but Mr Harris and Colonel Long went to his assistance and soon had them open.

It made little difference. The hot weather continued, and there was not a breath of a breeze to stir the heavy air. The garden was no less warm and airless than the room, and the Colonel, who had stepped outside after opening the door to look at the garden, commented that there was an unpleasantly brassy look to the sky.

'A good storm would not come amiss,' said Mr Jones, and was immediately cried down by the older ladies.

'I cannot abide thunder,' protested Mrs Calvert.

'Indeed no, and a heavy rain would lay the corn!' Miss

Enston contributed, and Mrs Willoughby, a lugubrious lady who always wore unrelieved black, said mournfully, 'Heavy rain reminds me of those dreadful monsoons. You may recall, Mr Harris, how enervating the rainy season becomes?'

'I had thought,' Mr Harris replied, looking puzzled, 'that the hot season was the more enervating, and the coming of the rains a relief, but no doubt continual torrential rain can become very enervating after a few days. I have no personal experience of a monsoon, however.'

'But were you not in India?' cried Mrs Willoughby, looking at him as though he had gained the honour of her acquaintance by means of false pretences.

'I'm afraid not,' he admitted apologetically.

'But you *have* been in Jamaica,' Miss Enston said triumphantly, 'and I dare say it is much the same there!'

Mr Harris was taken aback for a moment, no doubt wondering whether he should agree politely, or embark on a geography lesson, but Monsieur Roland, who had been sitting quietly in a corner, saying nothing and listening to all the conversations around him, said gently, 'Monsoons are peculiar to the shores of the Indian Ocean, but a similar heavy seasonal rainfall is experienced in the Caribbean, I believe.'

'Quite so.' Mr Harris smiled at him. 'You have been to the West Indies, sir?'

'No,' replied Monsieur Roland flatly, thereby killing a promising topic of conversation.

'My dear husband,' Mrs Willoughby began portentiously, and continued with a detailed account of Mr Willoughby's career with the East India Company, which was only terminated by the appearance of Mr Gibbs, the sexton, in the guise of a butler, to announce that dinner was served.

Mrs Calvert had given considerable thought to the planning of her dinner-table, and had contrived the seating, she believed, rather cleverly. As guest of honour, Mr Harris, of course, went in with his hostess and sat on her right, and Mr Calvert took in Mrs Willoughby, for she was the senior lady present in years and, at least in her own estimation, in rank as well, if her late husband's position in the hierarchy of 'John Company' was set against the comparative rank of Colonel Long. Mr Jones, as a mere curate, was expected to take in the least desirable partner, and found himself on Mrs Calvert's left with Miss Enston. Monsieur Roland could safely be given Mrs Long, who could speak a little French, which should be a comfort for him, and who was seated on her host's left, opposite Mrs Willoughby. This left Colonel Long to go in with Lucinda, and as he was an easy-going gentleman, he could sit next to Mrs Willoughby, thus placing Lucinda neatly on Mr Harris's right. It was unfortunate, Lucinda thought, that she was also opposite Miss Enston, who was unlikely to miss a single world, glance, nuance of expression or change of colour, and for the first time in her life she was unsure of her ability to control all those things with Mr Harris so close beside her. Her cheeks were already flushed from the heat, despite Mrs Calvert's bold decision to have the dining-room french doors open as well as those in the parlour.

During the first course, Mr Harris was naturally engaged in conversation with Mrs Calvert, and Lucinda with Colonel Long, but he was an undemanding partner and did little more than reply briefly to Lucinda's remarks while consuming his *soupe á la Julienne*, a baked trout with salad, and a little roast mutton. Mrs Willoughby was explaining the Hindu religion to the Rector and Monsieur Roland was showing a polite interest in Mrs

Long's kindly endeavours to help the young soldiers under her husband's command to send letters home to their families, for most of them could not write. Miss Enston was obviously listening to all the conversations, and at the same time eliciting from Mr Jones an account of his recent visit to his parents in Bedfordshire.

When the covers were removed for the second course, Mrs Calvert turned to Mr Jones, and everyone else obediently began a new conversation with the person sitting on the other side of them.

'I believe you've been to Austria?' Lucinda began, too rapidly and too bluntly.

'Now, I wonder who told you that?' Mr Harris replied without answering. 'Perhaps I can guess. Have you noticed how some people manage to learn a great deal about a newcomer within five minutes of his arrival, yet others can be acquainted with a person for years and still know not a thing about him?'

Lucinda was not sure what to make of these remarks, or how to reply, for she had a distressing feeling that she had been gently snubbed, so she said nothing and helped herself to cold roast duck, green peas and endive in silence, while Mr Harris took rabbit pie, artichokes and buttered new potatoes.

'I'll let you into a secret!' he said very quietly.

Lucinda automatically glanced at Miss Enston, but she seemed to be expounding with great intensity to Monsieur Roland on the last major explosion at the powder-mill.

'I was in Austria for about two years, but I had to leave in a hurry,' Mr Harris continued, as he speared a particularly rounded and well buttered potato and ate it with relish.

'Oh dear!' Lucinda said, wondering if she was about to hear some scandalous tale of crime, or a matter of an irate husband, or possibly even a duel. 'What happened?'

'An Italianate Frenchman arrived with an army and occupied Vienna,' Mr Harris replied calmly. 'As he entered by one road, I left by one on the opposite side of the city. It was very inconvenient.'

'Yes, it must have been.' Lucinda hesitated, a question hovering on the tip of her tongue.

'Now you may ask me what I was doing there,' he said encouragingly.

'What were you doing in Vienna?' Lucinda decided to treat it as a joke, although she was not at all sure that it was meant to be.

'I took some lessons in the Spanish Riding School, which is a rare privilege.' After a pause, he commented, 'This is a very good rabbit pie—where do you get your rabbits?'

Lucinda's cheeks reddened suddenly, for she knew very well who brought the rabbits to the kitchen door, and where he snared them, but she could hardly pass on the information to Mr Harris.

'Ah!' said that gentleman, looking at her sidelong. 'I suppose it's one of those unmentionable subjects, like the source of this excellent wine!'

'As a matter of fact,' Lucinda grasped at a safe subject, 'that wine is made from some apples which Mrs Martin gave us last autumn. Father claims it's as good as French wine, and he'll be pleased to hear that you mistook it for such!'

Mr Harris laughed, and raised his glass in a silent toast to her.

'If you wish for some of the other,' Lucinda went on quietly, 'I could tell you whom to ask. You're not a Preventive Officer in disguise, are you?' The question was not serious, but she was hesitant about giving information to a comparative stranger, which could get someone else into grave trouble, without at least a verbal reassurance.

'I have no connection with the Customs and Excise, except to evade them when I can, like everyone else,' he said solemnly. 'You need have no fear, however—I've already been approached about a certain matter by a certain blacksmith.'

Lucinda was very surprised to hear this, for she had never before known Will Plomer to 'approach' anyone in the way of illegitimate trade. Normally he waited until a newcomer had been in the town for at least a year, and then expected them to approach him, through an established customer.

While she was puzzling over this phenomenon, Annie brought in raspberry pies and trifle. There should have been cream to go with them, but Annie confided to Mrs Calvert in a hissing whisper that the cream had turned and Cook had substituted custard, but Lucinda, when she tasted it, suspected that the milk might have been on the turn as well. No one else appeared to notice, however, perhaps because they were distracted by the entry of a large dish of strawberry fritters, which were Cook's speciality, made to her secret recipe, and much admired by everyone who had ever had the good fortune to taste one.

For dessert, there were more strawberries, raspberries, the last of the cherries, raisins, nuts and a melon, and as it seemed to be getting hotter, if anything, instead of the more usual evening coolness, Mr Calvert proposed that they should all take their wine, tea or coffee in the garden. There a variety of seats had been put out during dinner—a rustic bench, some Windsor armchairs from the parlour, and the Rectory's three cane chairs, and Mrs Calvert's hammock-sofa was swinging under the walnut tree.

To Lucinda's surprise, even her mother found this idea agreeable, so they all removed outside, with a great deal of chattering and apparent excitement from the two older ladies, to whom the idea seemed quite novel. Lucinda remained behind for a moment to consult with Annie about the supper arrangements, for she feared that the cream turning sour might have affected them, but the maid assured her that Cook had everything in hand, and bustled out with a pile of plates to the kitchen. As she went, Monsieur Roland re-entered from the garden and whispered in a conspiratorial fashion, 'Miss Calvert! A word in your ear, if you please.'

'By all means,' she replied encouragingly, for she had a liking for the melancholy Frenchman, and assumed that something was troubling him. 'How may I help you?'

'It's rather I who may 'elp you!' he announced, managing to sound portentous, even in a whisper. 'A word of warning, Miss Calvert—don't trust this Mr 'Arris! I suspect there is something not altogether right about 'im.'

'Oh, surely not, m'sieur!' Lucinda protested, then checked herself, feeling that she was flying to Mr Harris's defence too readily. 'He seems a very pleasant gentleman.'

'Maybe,' was the cautious reply, 'but I'm sure I 'ave seen 'im before. I was in Paris on business for a few weeks during the Peace of Amiens, and I'm sure I saw 'im there, in a very suspicious place. I mean to challenge 'im on it, and see what 'e says! You mark my words—'e will lie.'

Lucinda was a little bewildered by his certainty, for she could see no reason why Mr Harris should not have been in Paris during the Peace—after all, hundreds of English people had taken the opportunity to visit France during those few months (and many had cause to regret it, for they were still there, as Bonaparte's prisoners). She made only a vague reply and went out into the garden, where she found her mother and Mrs Willoughby dispensing tea and coffee, with Mr Jones and Mr Harris handing the cups and becoming confused over who wished for tea, and who for coffee.

There was a heavy stillness in the garden. The birds had ceased to sing; even the swifts, who would usually be darting busily about the church eaves, shrilling as if in excitement, had fallen silent. Not a leaf was stirring in the trees, and the sky had a leaden look instead of the clear, sun-filled azure aspect it had worn earlier in the day.

'I fear the storm is approaching rapidly,' Mr Harris observed, presenting a cup of coffee to Lucinda.

'Thank you,' she replied, 'see, Fred agrees with you— There he goes!' And the stout black cat danced across the grass, hardly touching paw to ground, his tail, like a bottle-brush, held at an oblique angle, and ran up the trunk of the mulberry tree. Almost immediately he ran along one of the lower branches, sending ripe fruit showering to the ground, dived off the end of it, then walked sedately over to sniff Mr Harris's ankles and rub his head lovingly against them. Mr Harris bent to scratch him behind his ears, but after a few moments he leapt in the air and danced across to the border, where he rolled violently in a patch of nepeta.

'I suppose the electricity in the air has a galvanic effect on his fur,' said Mr Harris. 'I know my own hair crackles when I comb it in thundery weather.'

'Mine even sparks when I brush it!' Lucinda observed.

'One might make a laboured joke about that being due to its fiery colour'—Mr Harris's ironic smile was in evidence—'but you might think that derogatory to one of your most beautiful features, and I'd not wish you to misunderstand me!'

Lucinda was forced to stop and consider this speech, but before she had reached the conclusion that it was, in fact, a compliment, Monsieur Roland joined them, and said, apparently quite casually, 'I've just remembered where I saw you before, Mr 'Arris. I knew your face was familiar to me!'

'And where was that?' The riposte sounded a little sharp.

'In Paris,' he announced with an oddly defiant note in his voice.

'Then, Monsieur Roland, I regret to inform you that you're mistaken,' Mr Harris replied pleasantly. 'I've never been in Paris.'

'In the autumn of '02, in the Place de la Révolution,' he insisted, but Mr Harris, still smiling, shook his head. 'Coming out of the 'ouse of Talleyrand!' Monsieur Roland added with a flourish.

'You must have seen someone resembling me.' Mr Harris sounded quite unruffled. 'I was in Sweden from the summer of '02 to the late spring of '03.'

The Frenchman gave a very Gallic shrug, as if accepting that he was mistaken, but he also caught Lucinda's eye with a very significant look, as if to say, 'I told you so', and she was left feeling puzzled and uneasy.

'What were you doing in Sweden?' she asked, more for something to say than as a real enquiry, just to cover the awkward pause as Monsieur Roland sauntered away.

'Oh, this and that,' he replied vaguely, looking after him with a slight frown. 'Tell me: if you were walking past a house—say in Bruton Street—and a man you'd never seen before came out of it, would you be able to recognise him nearly five years later?'

'I doubt it.' Lucinda also looked at Monsieur Roland, who was now talking to Colonel Long. 'But why should he say he saw you, and that he remembers you, if he doesn't?'

'Goodness knows!' Mr Harris shrugged the matter aside. 'Now, when may I hope to go riding with you and the charming Miss Martin? I've two good mares, both broken to side-saddle, eating their heads off in my stables, and much in need of exercise.'

'Oh. I'd not thought you serious!' Lucinda exclaimed. 'I shall see Amy—Miss Martin—tomorrow, and perhaps we can arrange it. When would be suitable for you?'

'Is Friday a possibility?'

'Well—I do my sick-visiting in the morning, but I dare say the afternoon would be. If Amy is free, that is.'

'Then I'll send my groom to enquire on Thursday, and if you are both so minded, I'll bring the horses down after luncheon on Friday, and you shall show me the countryside. Perhaps I'll ask Captain Bridges to join us.'

'Thank you!' Lucinda smiled gratefully at him, for she had sorely missed riding since her old pony died. He moved a fraction closer to her, looking down into her upraised face, and their eyes met and held for what seemed to Lucinda an age, but was probably no more than a couple of seconds. A peculiar shiver ran through her body, and she found it difficult to breathe properly.

'Lucinda?' He barely whispered her name.

'I fear the storm is almost on us,' Mr Jones exclaimed from close behind Lucinda, making her start and swing round. 'Do you think it would be politic to go inside?'

'We'll have a little warning before the heavens open,' Mr Harris observed lightly, 'and it's a fraction cooler out here than it is within doors, I believe.'

'Yes.' Mr Jones squinted at the sky, which was now a

leaden colour, growing blacker every minute. 'I suppose the estimable Fred will give us warning of imminent rain—he seems content to race about in the open at present.'

Fred was, indeed, dancing again, and at one moment actually chased his own tail, which was twice its normal thickness, but suddenly, with a sharp 'Yow!', he fled indoors.

Immediately a gust of wind swept round the garden, making the upper branches of the trees lash about, raining mulberries, and slamming one leaf of the parlour french window with a crash. Miss Enston uttered a little shriek and clutched her cap, as the lappets rose and flapped like wings; Mrs Willoughby, with an audible and indignant cluck, rose in a dignified fashion and went to go into the house, the effect being unfortunately spoiled by her shawl, which rose like a black banshee and dropped over her head. She, too, uttered a small scream, and Colonel Long gallantly went to her rescue, but received little thanks, for he disarranged her elaborate lace cap in the process.

The wind dropped as suddenly as it had arisen, and a long growl of thunder reverberated through the heavy air. There was an agitation of birds about the church roof, which died away again quickly, and then a vivid streak of lightning lanced across the sky, making Lucinda blink.

'I don't like this!' Mr Harris sounded irritable. 'Lightning without rain is dangerous after so long a dry spell. If anything is struck, it will burn!'

'Indeed.' Mr Jones flinched as another flash of lightning exploded through the blackness above them. 'I think, Rector, I should wheel the fire-engine out from the porch on to the forecourt. It may be needed.'

The end of his sentence was almost drowned by the

crash of thunder, and lightning and more thunder came together, again and again, as Mrs Calvert and Mrs Long both retired hastily into the dining-room, where Mrs Willoughby was endeavouring to drape her shawl over the mirror above the fireplace.

'Come on—Rain, damn you!' Mr Harris apostrophised the sky.

There was another flash of lightning so brilliant that Lucinda shut her eyes and turned her head away in a reflex action, and on its heels came a violent crack.

'Something's struck!' cried Colonel Long, hastening towards the garden gate.

As he did so, shouting could be heard in the distance, and as the other men and Lucinda followed the Colonel, a nearer voice shouted, 'Fire! Fetch the engine! Fire!'

CHAPTER FIVE

'IS THE CHURCH locked?' asked the Rector.

'I don't know—I'll see.' Mr Jones was already running through the gate, pulling his keys from his pocket as he went.

'Come, John!' cried the Colonel. 'Let's lend a hand!' But Mr Harris was already passing him at a run to follow Mr Jones, the Rector not far behind, and the Colonel went with them.

Lucinda followed as far as the gate, then realised that her mother was probably unaware of what was happening and turned back to tell her. She collided with Monsieur Roland, who was standing as if rooted to the spot, wringing his hands nervously.

'I—I 'ave a dread of *le feu*,' he said, his English deteriorating in his agitation. '*Je ne peux pas*—I am not able . . .'

'There'll be more than enough people to help,' Lucinda said, her voice half-drowned in the rumble of the thunder. 'Please, come into the house. The ladies will be glad of your presence, for I'm sure they'll all be nervous.'

She took his arm and propelled him into the parlour, partly because it was the nearest way into the house, and partly to save him from Miss Enston's curious gaze until he had regained his self-control, for he was trembling. She turned to pull the french doors shut and wrestled with the stiff catch, while he stood in the middle of the room, apparently unaware that she needed help.

Another flash of lightning illumined a figure which had suddenly appeared outside the window and was trying to pull it open again. Lucinda, having just succeeded in fastening the catch, was obliged to wrench at it again to unfasten it, and Mr Harris, for it was he, impatiently pulled it open and thrust a bundle into her arms.

'Coats,' he said succinctly. 'Shan't need them. Put 'em somewhere, there's a good girl. It's a house in the market square that's struck—burning merrily, and likely to spread. All timber-framed, I suspect,' and he was gone, his white shirt gleaming in the lightning, which was now less fierce, for the storm was rapidly passing over.

'What's happening?' Mrs Calvert asked sharply, coming into the parlour from the hall, with the other ladies behind her. 'Where have the gentlemen gone?'

'There's a house on fire in the market square,' Lucinda explained, putting the bundle of coats down on a chair. 'Mr Harris says it's burning fiercely, and likely to spread.'

'Hm.' Mrs Calvert paused to consider, suddenly transformed into the capable manager whom the Rector had married. 'Ladies!'—turning towards the female guests—'May I ask your help? There may be injured folk, and certainly there'll be some needing shelter. Will you fetch bandages and salves from the still-room—Miss Enston, you know where it is—will you and Mrs Long fetch the large wooden box on the window-sill, and the jars marked "burns". Mrs Willoughby, will you come with me to fetch blankets? Lucinda, run up to the fire and tell your father to send anyone in need of help down here as quickly as possible. Oh, and do you stay there, and see to anyone who may be frightened, especially the children. Comfort them, you know, and send them down.' She swept out, carrying the other ladies before her.

'Yes, Mama.' Lucinda went towards the door in her wake, then checked and turned back to say, 'Monsieur Roland, would you please hang those coats on the backs of the chairs, to save them from creasing? Colonel's Long's in particular, for that scarlet crumples abominably.'

'Indeed.' He pulled himself together. 'And then I shall 'elp Mrs Calvert.'

'Yes. Thank you,' Lucinda replied absently, already making for the front door, and it banged behind her a moment later.

As soon as she rounded the bulk of the church, the whereabouts of the fire became apparent, for a column of smoke shot through by sparks and flames was ascending from the market square, and it glowed a vivid red above the dark roofs. She ran up the churchyard path and through the arch, and came upon a luridly lit scene of activity.

It seemed that half the townspeople were there, crowded along the east side of the square, watching open-mouthed as the tallow-chandler's shop on the west side blazed. Flames and smoke were pouring through its roof and from the windows on the topmost of its three storeys, and an ominous glow was lighting those on the first floor.

The fire-engine, a long, box-like object on wheels, was standing before the burning house, and Mr Jones and the Rector, hindered rather than helped by Mr Palmer, the chandler, were busily uncoiling a hose from one end, while Mr Harris and Colonel Long worked on the one at the other end. A dozen men were standing by the pump-handles—long poles running lengthwise, one on either side of the box, which must be thrust down alternately to pump water in through one hose and out through the other.

The two clergymen had the intake hose, and as soon as it was unwound, they ran with the end of it through the carriage-arch between the burning house and its neighbour, in order to drop it down the well in the back yard of one or the other. As soon as they returned, the men fell to pumping as hard as they could, and presently an uncertain jet of water came from the other hose, which Mr Harris and the Colonel directed at the burning house.

'Is there a good depth of water?' Mr Harris shouted.

'Yes, it's a deep well!' Mr Calvert shouted back.

Lucinda watched, awed by the power of the fire, for it could not have been more than fifteen minutes since the lightning struck, yet already the upper two floors were a solid mass of flame, and the single hose seemed to have no effect at all.

Mr Palmer, at last seeing that his attempts to help were more trouble than they were worth, was standing with his two servants, wringing his hands and looking distraught. He was an elderly widower, and Lucinda felt very sorry for him, and was relieved when his son appeared and gently led him away to his own home near by, the servants following.

· The men at the pumps were swiftly and efficiently relieved by another team as their pace began to flag, and two more men took over the hose. Lucinda grasped the opportunity to deliver her mother's message to the Rector, and then her arm was taken by Mr Harris, who pulled her away to a safer distance from the fire.

'What are you doing here?' he asked, sounding disapproving.

'Mama sent me to tell my father to send the injured or

homeless to the Rectory. Oh, look! The next house has caught!'

Mr Harris, who had been standing with his back to the fire, swung round, looked, and said grimly, 'It's run along the roof timbers, I expect. We need another pump and hose. Is that the only one?'

'There's one at the powder-mill, but they're not allowed to lend it,' Lucinda replied. 'Would buckets . . .?'

'Good girl! A bucket chain!' Mr Harris ran across to the crowd of watchers and shouted, 'All of you—Run home and fetch buckets! Make a chain to the nearest well! We need more than one hose!'

For a moment, most of the crowd stood and gaped at him uncomprehendingly, and then light dawned on the more quick-witted and they began to hurry away, the word 'buckets' being bandied back and forth until everyone seemed to grasp the idea, and they all ran off in various directions.

Lucinda turned back to the fire, and saw that the roof of the second building was alight, with tiles exploding from the roof with sharp reports. It was the draper's shop, and, after staring for a moment, she realised who lived there, on the attic floor, and looked about wildly for Mr Harris, saw he had gone back to the pump, ready to take a turn, and ran to him.

'John! Mr Harris!' she cried, clutching his arm.

He turned, startled. 'Don't come near!' he exclaimed, pulling her back, away from the fire. 'The front could fall at any time now.'

'That house—the second one!' She was shaking his arm to hold his attention. 'Duke Howe lives there. He's in bed, on the top floor, with a broken ankle. He won't be able to get out!'

Mr Harris looked at her, his face grim, then turned

towards the house, the top floor of which was blazing.

'Very well,' he said, 'Stay here!' and he ran, shouting, 'There's someone in there!' as he passed the fire-engine. The men with the hose had turned the jet towards the second house, for the first was clearly beyond saving, and the spray fell on him, soaking him briefly before he charged the shop door, burst it open, and disappeared inside.

Lucinda, horrified, clasped her hands over her mouth, and thought, 'Please God! *Please!* Oh, please God!' over and over again, but she was distracted by a sudden outburst of screaming from a woman who had just come running from the churchyard arch, across the square towards the burning buildings. It was Mrs Howe.

'Duke! My son! My son's in there! Oh God, help me! Somebody help!' She seemed about to rush into the building, but Lucinda darted forward and seized her arms, holding her back with all her strength.

'Mr Harris is gone in for him!' she shouted, shaking the woman and repeating the words until she understood them. It took a few minutes, but the reiteration eventually penetrated her understanding and she turned to look at Lucinda, then stopped pulling against her and allowed herself to be drawn away to a safe distance, where she stood staring towards the open door, tears pouring down her face.

By now, people were running back into the square with buckets, and Mr Morris of the Wyvern, which was next door to the draper's, pushed and pulled them into a line from the pump in the far corner of the square to as close to the fire as possible, and soon a chain of people was passing full buckets along, splashing half the water out of them until they got into the proper swing of things, and speeding empty buckets back again. The effect on the fire was minimal, but at least they could feel that they

were doing something. Lucinda thought absently that
she had never seen such a variety of buckets—tin,
leather, wood, iron, canvas, some leaking, others too
big or too heavy to be completely filled . . .

It was only the vaguest of impressions, and it was not
until after it was all over that she remembered noticing at
all; at the time, her attention, like Mrs Howe's, was
riveted on that gaping doorway, where already flames
were flickering among the goods on the shelves and
counter. To make matters worse, the original fire had
reached the ground floor of the tallow-chandler's, and
his highly flammable stock erupted into a great mass of
white-hot flame, roaring like a furnace, the sudden
increase of heat sending the pumpers and the hose-men
staggering back to escape being scorched.

Suddenly a strangely deformed figure, a monstrous
hunchback, appeared in the draper's doorway and
staggered out into the open. At once a well-meaning
member of the bucket chain flung the contents of a full
bucket over the figure, and half a dozen men ran to its
assistance, and it was only then that Lucinda realised
that it was Mr Harris, carring Marmaduke Howe across
his shoulders.

Mrs Howe ran to her son, who was lowered until he
could stand shakily on his sound foot, supported by two
of the men who had been pumping. He seemed to be
more bewildered than hurt, and was shaking his head
and trying to answer the chorus of voices asking him how
he felt, if he was hurt, and how he got out of the attic, as
he was carried away towards the archway by his friends,
his mother fussing about him as they went.

Lucinda changed her prayer to a heartfelt one of
thanks, closing her eyes as she did so, and was surprised,
when she opened them, to find that Mr Harris had
arrived beside her and was slapping at smouldering

patches on his shirt, which now sported several holes with black edges.

'You're burned!' she exclaimed.

'Well, under the circumstances, what did you expect?' he asked a shade tartly. 'In fact, I'm only slightly scorched, and my shirt is ruined. Young Howe had the sense to drag himself down the stairs almost to the bottom, but the smoke half-choked him and he couldn't manage it any further. He's all right.'

There was a vivid flash of light, and both Lucinda and Mr Harris turned apprehensively towards the fire before they realised that it came from above, and a rumble of thunder heralded the approach of another storm.

'Now, this time, rain, damn you, *rain*!' he shouted heavenwards. 'The next building appears to be brick, or it would be burning by now. Nevertheless, I doubt we can stop the whole of this side of the square going, unless it rains. The well is pumped dry, and the buckets can't do much.'

Lucinda looked at the fire-engine with a feeling of sick horror, for she had always assumed that having it in the town would mean less fear of a fire spreading beyond one building, and might even make it possible to put out a fire before it took hold. She felt let down by the engine, which now stood, idle and forlorn, with the men who had been pumping standing about listlessly, powerless to stop the other buildings in the row from catching and burning in their turn. A few hopefuls were pulling at the intake hose, to bring it out of the apparent heart of the fire, perhaps thinking to try to make it reach to another well. The Rector and Mr Jones were obviously discussing which well to try for, as they were pointing in different directions and looking about as they talked.

The lightning flashed again, but the thunder which followed it passed unnoticed, for at that moment, there was a shout of alarm, and everyone scattered away from the fire as the whole of the front of the tallow-chandler's leaned slowly outwards, further and further, until it crashed in a mass of sparks and burning brands across the fire-engine and the area around it.

Something hot and fiery flew past Lucinda's face as Mr Harris flung his arms about her and threw her to the ground, coming down himself heavily on top of her and knocking most of the breath out of her body. She lay gasping for a few moments, desperately sucking air into her lungs, seeing pieces of burning wreckage falling all around, and felt Mr Harris give a sudden jerk as he said something which he would certainly not normally have uttered in a lady's presence.

Presently he rolled off Lucinda, and said in a more customary fashion, 'I'm sorry about that. I hope I didn't hurt you?'

'No,' she replied uncertainly, sitting up and thinking that she would probably have a number of bruises from the sudden violent contact with the granite setts which paved the market square. 'Thank you. Oh!'

The exclamation was caused by the feeling of something cold and wet hitting her in the face, and she looked up, only to receive a dozen or more repetitions of the sensation as the black clouds opened and a deluge of rain descended.

For once, it was received with pleasure. The fire-fighters positively capered with joy, for even the slowest-witted had realised that, without a miracle, they could not hope to prevent the fire from spreading along the whole of the west side of the market square, and perhaps even further—and the miracle had arrived!

Lucinda sat on the ground, cold rain soaking her soot-stained best gown, icy trickles running down her back and between her breasts, and watched, laughing with relief, as the flames slowly died down and the burning buildings turned to smouldering ruins. She was aware that Mr Harris was very close beside her, with his arm round her shoulders, pressing her against the hard warmth of his body, but that seemed perfectly natural and right, an entirely pleasurable circumstance, and she would have been content to sit there for some time, as the rain lashed down and the storm flashed and rumbled to and fro above her head.

Fortunately for her health's sake, Mr Harris emerged from his state of euphoria fairly rapidly, and got up, pulling her to her feet.

'My dear girl!' he exclaimed. 'You're soaked to the skin! Come—there's no more to do here, for the moment. Have you any salve for burns in your admirable Rectory, do you think?'

'Oh, you *are* burned!' Lucinda cried, returning to harsh reality. 'Come home quickly, and let me find something to ease it!' She took his hand and ran with him through the pouring rain, down the churchyard path, his long legs somehow adapting their stride to her shorter paces, which were hampered by the clinging wetness of her long skirts. He seemed in excellent condition, for he had breath enough to be humming a tune as he ran, which seemed an absurd thing to be doing under the circumstances.

They found a great bustle going on at the Rectory, for a number of people had been struck by flying wreckage when the building collapsed, most of it burning, and they had come to the Rectory for treatment and excited gossip about the evening's events. Most of the pumpers had blistered hands, and one man had tripped over the hose as he tried to run, and had a sprained ankle.

Duke Howe was there, enthroned on a sofa in the parlour, but his mother had abandoned him and was hard at work with Miss Enston, the other ladies and some of the townsmen, bathing, salving and bandaging, under the surprisingly energetic direction of Mrs Calvert.

Lucinda took Mr Harris to the kitchen, which was comparatively quiet as only Cook and Annie were there, brewing quantities of tea for the injured and anyone else who seemed in need of refreshment. Another wooden box containing bandages and a pot of salve was kept on a shelf near the range against cooking accidents, and Lucinda, instructing Mr Harris to sit down at the table, reached up and set it on the table in front of him.

'Now,' she said, surveying him, 'where are you hurt?'

The kitchen was not particularly well lit, having only a few candles alight, but, even so, she could see that his shirt was scorched and burnt in a number of places, and she hesitated, hardly knowing where to start.

'You should go and change your clothes first,' he said. 'You're soaked, and I'd not wish you to take a chill.'

'I'm quite warm, and I shall do very well,' she replied, although she had to admit to herself that she was far from comfortable. 'Where shall I start?'

'I'd best take my shirt off . . .' he began, but Lucinda took out the scissors from the box, inserted them into the hole over his shoulder, and slit the garment down the back, pulling the tails out of his breeches, until she could rip it right away from his body. She then cut the sleeves, and after he had taken off his cravat and collar, she soon had the rest of the garment off him.

None of the burns was particularly bad, but there were more than a dozen sore patches, which she gently anointed with salve, occasionally drawing a sharp intake of breath from him, but he made no other sound, even after Cook and Annie had clattered away with their tea-trays and there was only Lucinda to hear him. His upper right arm had caught the worst burn, a patch about two inches across which was blistered and weeping, and that she salved and bandaged with a strip of linen.

'There,' she said when she had finished. 'That should take the worst off, but you must let Dr Roberts look at the one I've bandaged, for it's blistered.' She stood back and looked at the sore places, anxiously trying to judge whether she had put sufficient salve on them, and only gradually becoming aware of the lean and muscular torso, and the broad shoulders tapering to narrow hips.

'Are you admiring your handiwork?' Mr Harris enquired, but not with any apparent innuendo. Lucinda, however, hastily moved behind him and went to wash her hands at the sink to hide her flushed cheeks.

'Would you care for a glass of wine, or perhaps some brandy?' she suggested, tidying the pot of salve and the remaining bandages away into their box.

'I'd prefer some tea, or ale, or even water,' he replied, moving his shoulders gingerly, as if to test the soreness of his burns. 'I'm parched!'

Cook and Annie had carried all the tea they had made to the parlour and dining-room, leaving not so much as a cup and dish behind, but there was a barrel of small ale in the pantry, kept for the servants, so Lucinda drew off a pint into a pewter tankard, which rightly belonged to Mr Gibbs, and Mr Harris drank it with relish and was not averse to another when it was offered.

'I think I'd better find you one of Father's shirts,' Lucinda said, still very much aware of his bare chest. 'Yours is quite beyond repair, I'm afraid.'

'Mm. You were a little drastic with the scissors,' he replied. 'Is the water in your pump good to drink? I'd best not have any more ale, or I might behave in an unseemly fashion!'

'Yes, it's drawn straight from our own well,' she assured him, and would have rinsed and filled his tankard for him, but he forestalled her and worked the little pump over the sink himself, while she ran upstairs to fetch him a shirt.

The whole of the ground floor of the house, apart from the kitchen, seemed to be full of people who were either having their injuries tended or helping, or just standing about talking excitedly about the evening's events. There was even a little group of men sitting on the stairs earnestly discussing how they could raise the money for a new fire-engine, and what improvements they would like to build into it after their experience with the old one. Lucinda picked her way through them and found a shirt. As she came down the stairs again, and they were shifting about to let her through, one of them, the ostler from the Black Swan, looked up at her and said encouragingly, 'Eh, dear, Miss Calvert! You look fair terrible!' He was immediately thumped by his friends and informed that that was no way to talk to a lady, and asked if he had no sense, adjured to choose his words more carefully, and thumped again severally for good measure.

Meanwhile, Lucinda negotiated the rest of the stairs and hurried back towards the kitchen. There was a mirror hanging on the wall above a small table near the kitchen door, where someone had put a lighted candle in a stick, so she paused for a moment to look at her reflection.

She hardly recognised herself. Her hair had slipped half-way down the back of her head, and one of her ringlets seemed to be only half the length it should have been. When she touched it, the ends felt curiously crimped and came away in her fingers in a sort of ash, and she realised that it must have been burned. Her face was streaked with soot, the lace collar at the neck of her gown was crumpled and stained, and her best gown . . .! She looked down at it and saw that it was filthy and torn, and obviously could never be worn again.

Mr Harris looked up as she re-entered and gave her a cheerful greeting, rubbing at his face and head with a kitchen towel, for he had obviously been washing. He took the shirt gratefully and got it over his head and his arms into the sleeves with a little help from Lucinda, and then said, 'Have you any idea where my coat might be? It seems to have stopped raining, and I'd like to go home before I drop in my tracks from exhaustion!'

'I expect it's in the parlour,' Lucinda replied, thinking that he did now look very tired. She went to look for the coat, and found that Monsieur Roland had done as she asked and the coats which Mr Harris had brought back, seemingly so long ago, were hung on the backs of chairs, although one or two had still managed to get themselves creased because people had been leaning on them. Mr Harris's, however, was quite presentable, and she managed to recover it and take it to him without being seen by her mother, who would probably have thrown a fit of strong hysterics at the sight of her in her present state.

Mr Harris eased himself into the garment cautiously, commenting that he could wish that his tailor had not made it quite such a perfect fit. Then he thanked her politely for her help in rather formal terms, which she found unexpected after his earlier easy, rather unconventional behaviour, and also oddly disappointing, and then he went to the back door, where he stood looking out.

'Not a cloud in the sky, and the night so full of stars there's hardly room for a bat to fly between them!'

'How will you get home?' Lucinda asked, wondering if she should invite him to stay the night, for there was a guest-room in the house.

'I left my carriage at the Swan,' he replied, 'and I sent a fellow round to tell my man to put the horses to while you were fetching the shirt. Try to get to bed before, long, m'dear—you look completely fagged! Good night, Miss Calvert, and thank you again.'

'Good night, Mr Harris,' she replied, and stood staring after him, long after he had disappeared into the night.

Then Annie came clattering into the kitchen with a loaded tray and exclaimed, 'They're all going off home now, thank goodness! Colonel Long wishes a word with you, if you wouldn't mind.'

Lucinda put a weary hand to her head and tried to push her hair into some approximation of order as she left the kitchen and went along to the hall, which seemed to be full of people saying 'Good night, then!' and thanking the Rector, who was standing by the front door.

Colonel Long was by the door of the Rector's study, watching for Lucinda, and he caught her attention by lifting one hand level with his head. She made her way over to him, and he drew her into the study and shut the door.

'I'm sorry to bother you, Miss Calvert,' he said. 'But it's quite important, and I don't wish to worry your parents about it, for they've enough to think of at present. You're a very sensible young lady, and I'm sure you'll help me admirably, if you'll be so kind.'

'Of course, Colonel, but what is it?' Lucinda asked anxiously.

'There were some papers in my coat-pocket earlier this evening,' he said, watching her face attentively.

'They were there when I gave my coat to John Harris to bring back with the others, but when I collected it from the parlour, the papers were missing.'

'You mean they were no longer in your pocket?' Lucinda said blankly, feeling too tired to think clearly. 'Perhaps they'd fallen out.'

'Most likely, but I looked about the parlour, as best I could without attracting attention, and couldn't see them. You didn't happen to notice them when Mr Harris gave you the coats, I suppose?'

Lucinda thought back to the incident, which now seemed so long ago. 'I didn't really notice anything,' she said, 'I took the coats from Mr Harris, and put them down, and I asked Monsieur Roland to hang them on the chairs. Then Mama asked me to go to the market square, and I ran off. Shall we go and search the parlour? They may have fallen out and been kicked under the furniture . . .'

'I think,' said the Colonel, 'if it's not asking too much, that I'd rather you had a look in the morning, when there's no one else about. It's difficult to see by candle-light, and someone is bound to ask what we're looking for if we do it now. It's a small packet of papers, only four or five sheets, folded to about four inches in either direction, with my name written on the outside.'

'Yes, of course I'll look. What shall I do if I find them?'

'Keep them safe. I'll call tomorrow, at about half-past eleven, to enquire how everyone is after tonight's doings, and perhaps you would give them to me then, or tell me if you don't find them. Er—I'd rather you didn't mention this to anyone else. I don't wish people to speculate and gossip about my carelessness!'

'I shan't say a word to anyone,' Lucinda assured him. 'But it might be an idea to ask Monsieur Roland if he saw them, if I don't find them, for I left the coats in his charge, you see.'

Colonel Long hesitated, then said, 'No, I'd rather not involve anyone else. I dare say they just fell out of the pocket at some point. Thank you very much, Miss Calvert, and I'll bid you good night now, for I must be keeping you from your bed.'

Lucinda saw him out, and exchanged a few words with her father, then went yawning up the stairs to her room, where she found that Annie had left her two big jugs of hot water so that she could wash the smell of smoke and the soot from herself and her hair, for which she was very grateful.

While she was combing out her damp hair, her mother came into the room in nightshift and wrappers, her carefully arranged coiffure protected by a lacy night-cap, and sank down exhaustedly on the edge of the bed.

'What an evening!' she exclaimed. 'I can hardly believe that it's not yet midnight!'

'Where did everyone go, in the end?' Lucinda enquired, fingering the ends of the burnt ringlet, and wondering what she should do about it.

'Apparently Mr Palmer, the chandler, went to his son's house,' Mrs Calvert replied through a small yawn, 'and the Howes are gone to her sister in Gold Street.'

'And what became of Monsieur Roland?' Lucinda made up her mind, and snipped off the frizzled ends of the burnt ringlet with her embroidery scissors, which happened to be lying on her dressing-table.

'He made himself useful for a time, and then simply went. I confess I was most disappointed in him, but your father says he is obviously much affected by thunder and lightning, and we must be . . . Mercy on us, Lucinda! What did you just do to your hair?'

'It was a little burnt when Mr Palmer's shop fell down,' Lucinda replied calmly. 'I was just trimming off the ends.'

Mrs Calvert uttered a cry of horror and groped in the pocket of one of her wrappers for her smelling-bottle, which she then waved under her nose for a few moments. 'You had no business to go so near!' she then scolded.

'I wasn't particularly close,' Lucinda protested mildly. 'But, you see, the whole front of the building fell forward, and pieces of burning timber were thrown across the market square, and that's why so many people had burns. Poor Mr Harris had his shirt quite ruined, so I lent him one of Father's. He had several burns about his arms and shoulders as well,' she added as something of an afterthought.

'I hear that he went into the fire to rescue Marmaduke Howe,' Mrs Calvert said pensively. 'That was a very brave thing to do.' She gave a little sigh. 'I do wish we knew more about him! He seems a pleasant man, but quite unresponsive to any—er—hinting about his background!'

'But I thought that the Longs were acquainted with him?' Lucinda made a great pretence of having nine-tenths of her attention on her curling-rags. 'Was he not at Cambridge with the Colonel's brother?'

'Only at the same time. Mrs Long says that they only met a few times, at university functions, for they were not members of the same college. The Colonel seems quite friendly with him, and your father called him a capital fellow . . . I do wish he would not use these colloquialisms—so unsuitable to a Man of the Cloth!'

'Fred likes him,' Lucinda pointed out defensively, but it was the wrong thing to say.

'One can hardly be guided in one's choice of friends by

the opinion of a cat!' Her mother's voice was scornful. 'Good night, Lucinda.' And with that, she gave her an offhand kiss and left the room.

Lucinda called 'Good night, Mama!' after her, finished curling her hair, pinched out her candles and climbed into bed. She felt bone-weary after the evening's excitements and expected to fall asleep at once, but somehow, after a few minutes, she was wide awake and not inclined to sleep at all.

Despite gloomy warnings from her mother, she slept with her windows open in the warm weather, and from her bed she could smell the scent of wet earth—of dusty wet earth, parched by several weeks of hot, dry weather, and now soaked by welcome rain. Mingled with it came the sweet scent of roses from the climber by her window, the cloying smell of honeysuckle, and the sound of a little breeze in the tree-tops.

It was all very peaceful, and a strange contrast to her experiences earlier in the evening during the fire, which she did not wish to think about, and in that strange little interlude afterwards, when she had sat on the ground in the pouring rain with Mr Harris's arm round her, watching the fire splutter into extinction in the lurid flashes of lightning. She supposed that much of the feeling of contentment which she had felt then had been due to the relief of seeing the fire put out before any more damage had been done, and without anyone being seriously injured, but she had to admit that part of it had been concerned with the nearness of Mr Harris, the hard warmth of his body against her, and the clasp of his arm round her shoulders.

'But I've known him only a week!' she whispered aloud. Could a person actually fall in love with someone in a week? In romantic novels, perhaps, but surely not in real life! Besides, she disliked several things about him—the way he sometimes seemed to be laughing at her, the hard, calculating look in his eyes which she had glimpsed once or twice, and his evasiveness when one tried to glean information about his past . . .

There had been that odd conversation with Monsieur Roland, too. Why had the Frenchman been so sure that he had seen him in Paris, and in a specific place which seemed to have some significance so deep that Monsieur Roland could remember the incident nearly five years later? Yet Mr Harris had said that he was not in Paris then, had never been there, but in—where was it— Sweden? What on earth could he have been doing there, for the Swedes had not been at all friendly to British people at that time. It all seemed very mysterious.

Lucinda tossed and turned, her thoughts becoming more and more confused as she tried to make sense of the few facts she had gleaned about Mr Harris, and set them alongside the things she was sure she disliked about him, and her undoubtedly strong feeling of physical attraction to him. It was as if her mind and body had formed two quite different opinions of the man, and she hardly knew what to make of the situation. Suddenly her tiredness caught up with her, and she fell asleep.

There was no danger of anyone oversleeping in Woodham, for Mr Gibbs rang the apprentice bell every morning, except Sundays, sharp at six. This was later than in most towns where the old custom was still kept up, but it had been decided at a vestry meeting some years before that five was unnecessarily early. He varied the bell on which he actually rang, but never used Gabriel, for he was the passing bell, and the sexton probably thought it would be depressing for folk to be woken by those deep tones. On the morning after the fire, he chose Michael, the number six, so there was certainly no possibility of Lucinda not waking, which was as she wished, for she had decided to look for Colonel Long's papers before anyone else entered the parlour.

The room was unusually untidy, for most of the injured from the fire had been treated here, and the furniture was pushed about out of its usual places. Lucinda replaced chairs and tables in their proper order as she searched, looking under cushions, thrusting her hands down between the backs and seats of the two sofas, peering behind and under all the pieces which were too heavy to move. She found a number of items, from odd playing-cards to a brooch which her mother had lost quite a year before, but not Colonel Long's papers.

When she was quite sure they were not in the room, she went out into the garden to look there. It was another fine, sunny day, but not as oppressively hot as the past week had been. Raindrops still glistened on the leaves, and the grass was wet where the sunlight had not yet reached it, but the sky was blue, the swifts were flying high above the church, and Fred was sunning himself on the stone path near the vegetable patch.

Lucinda walked slowly to the gate, looking about her, peering under bushes and clumps of flowers, and then surveyed the paved forecourt in front of the church door. She even walked to the corner and looked up the churchyard path, and went into the porch to look in the dark corners, but nowhere could she see anything resembling the Colonel's papers.

She dismissed them from her thoughts during breakfast, at which Mrs Calvert did not appear, being still asleep, and the Rector was absorbed in some calculations which he had made on an odd scrap of paper about the probable cost of a new fire-engine.

'We shall have to do a great deal of praying over this,' he said. 'Both the buildings destroyed in the fire were insured, thank heaven, but I think we must have a public subscription, for I'm sure all the goods lost could not have been covered—the Howes' belongings, in particular. Oh dear!'

'Remember Elijah and the ravens, Father!' Lucinda said encouragingly.

'Indeed!' The Rector beamed over his spectacles at her. 'We must trust in the Lord to send us some very large and deep-pocketed ravens, and I must be off, for Mr Jones and I are to go into London this morning to see the insurance people, and bespeak a new fire-engine.'

After he had gone, Lucinda received a succession of visitors, headed by Miss Enston who was agog to hear about Lucinda's experiences at the fire. Then came Mrs Willoughby, Mrs Martin, and two or three others, all to enquire after Mrs Calvert following her exhausting evening, and to offer help in reclothing and re-equipping the folk who had lost their homes. Fortunately none of them stayed more than the customary ten minutes for a morning call. They were followed by Monsieur Roland, who came informally by way of the garden gate and the french doors to the parlour, saying apologetically, 'I come for a few seconds only to express my sorrow for my uselessness last night. I'm deeply ashamed that my fear of fire and thunder combined to make me so—what do you say?—spineless!'

'Think nothing of it, Monsieur Roland,' Lucinda said encouragingly. 'And don't say another word about it, for no one holds it against you.'

Of course, he said many more words about it, but then he, too, went away, again by the way of the garden, and just as Lucinda had decided to visit Amy Martin and was shutting the french doors preparatory to leaving, Mr

Harris arrived outside them, just as he had done the previous night.

'I'll not stay above a minute, for I've no doubt you've been plagued by long-nosed shrews all morning; and I trust you'll forgive my coming through the garden, but I thought it best not to ring the door bell, in case your mother is resting,' he said hurriedly. 'Here's your father's shirt—it's been washed and ironed. Also, my thanks for your ministrations last night. I've seen Dr Roberts this morning, as you instructed, and he's put some more stuff on the burns, but not nearly as gently as you did. You're a grand girl, Lucinda!' and, with that, he thrust the Rector's shirt into her hands, bent to kiss her lightly on the cheek, and was gone before she could say anything.

For a few moments, she stood with one hand touching her cheek, where his kiss still burned, and the other pressing the shirt to her breast, and creasing it quite horridly in the process, and then she wandered absent-mindedly into the garden, gazing unseeingly at the ground before her feet. It was several seconds before she noticed, hardly two yards from the parlour doors, a small packet of papers lying under a bushy peony.

CHAPTER SIX

'IT CERTAINLY wasn't there an hour before,' Lucinda assured Colonel Long when she told him about finding the packet.

'You're sure?' he asked, his normally placid face looking quite stern.

'Yes, I am. I searched most carefully here, in the parlour, and then along the way Mr Harris must have come with the coats yesterday evening. I must have seen the packet, had it been there. Besides, it was quite dry, so it couldn't have been there during the rain! Is it a very serious matter?'

'No, not at all,' the Colonel replied a shade too quickly. 'It's just that it would have been inconvenient to lose the papers. I'm most grateful to you, Miss Calvert. Er—you've not mentioned it to anyone?'

'No, of course not. You asked me not to,' Lucinda replied with a trace of indignation.

'Excellent. Pray continue to keep it to yourself. Not a whisper even to your friend Miss Martin, eh?'

'Very well.' Lucinda smiled. 'I learn a great many secrets, you know, for people often talk to me about their problems. I suppose they think that the Rector's daughter is also bound by the seal of the confessional!'

'Ha-hum! Precisely.' Colonel Long nodded. 'And you feel no ill-effects of last night, I trust? You weren't struck by any of the burning wreckage?'

The sudden change of subject was occasioned by the sound of Mrs Calvert's voice in the hall, addressing a remark to Annie, and she then wandered in, looking frail and languid, and collapsed gracefully on to a sofa.

'Good morning, Colonel,' she said faintly. 'What an ordeal! I'm quite exhausted, and I wonder to see you abroad at all, after your prodigious exertions.'

'Good morning, ma'am.' The Colonel bowed and resumed the seat from which he had risen as she entered. 'All in a night's work, so to speak, for the army, you know! I was sorry to hear you're not feeling up to snuff this morning, for you were a tower of strength last night—a veritable tower! Mrs Long was filled with admiration; she says a Commissariat-General couldn't have managed matters with more efficiency.'

Mrs Calvert acknowledged this complimentary speech with a weak smile, raising one languid hand, and letting it fall again as if she had not the strength to support it. 'One does what one can,' she murmured.

After the Colonel had taken his leave, however, she rallied sufficiently to go into luncheon and make a good meal, but retired afterwards to her hammock seat, wrapped carefully in an array of shawls and rugs. Lucinda set off on her postponed visit to Amy, who greeted her in the garden with a fusillade of questions and exclamations about the events of the previous evening.

'We missed it all,' she explained. 'Papa took us over to Horsing, to spend the evening with my aunt and uncle, and we stayed late because of the storm, so it was all over by the time we returned.'

Lucinda gave her a somewhat bald account of the fire, and was self-consciously careful not to make much mention of Mr Harris, but she could not gloss over his gallant rescue of Duke Howe, even if she had wished to do so.

'Oh, how magnificent! I find your Mr Harris most admirable. Do you not admire him, Lucy? Confess, now—do you not find him handsome and agreeable and quite nobly heroic?'

'I suppose so,' Lucinda replied prosaically, 'but I could wish he were not so—so secretive.'

'Secretive!' exclaimed Amy. 'Oh, come now! A little reticent, perhaps, but only showing a proper modesty! Would you have him tell everyone his entire life's history at a first meeting?' She reflected for a moment, then added, 'I believe he teases a little when people are curious. I think you are very intrigued by him. Come, now—confess!'

'He makes me feel . . .' Lucinda groped for the word, 'uneasy.' It was not quite what she meant, but Amy appeared to understand, for she nodded sagely, and said, 'You'd best watch out, Lucy, or you'll be in love with him before you know where you are!'

'Oh, nonsense!' Lucinda protested, but she was beginning to suspect that Amy might be right. 'What do you know of being in love?' It seemed safer to carry the battle to the enemy in this matter.

'I know very well.' Amy's eyes wandered past her friend and gazed unseeingly across the garden. 'First, one feels ill at ease in his presence, self-conscious, anxious about his opinion of what one says and does. One's cleverest remarks seem suddenly to sound uncommonly foolish, and nothing goes as one had planned . . . Then it begins to appear that the sun shines only when one is near him, even if it's raining, and a day like today'—gesturing towards the cloudless sky—'is dull and overcast because *he* is not there. One resorts to childish stratagems to see him—walking where *he* is likely to pass, manufacturing excuses to speak to him, and if all goes well when one is with him, and the conversation runs smoothly, and his attention doesn't wander to other things and people . . . Oh, Lucy, it's so wonderful! Even ten minutes of such bliss is something golden, something to treasure and gloat over!'

Lucinda watched her friend's face with anxious attention, and then said bluntly, 'If it's Mr Jones, he hardly took his eyes off you in church last Sunday.'

'Mr Jones!' Amy returned to normality with a jerk. 'Why, whatever makes you think I was talking of myself and—and anyone? Look, Lucy, how much I've collected for the Cob-Enders today. I was out all morning, begging and persuading.' She gestured towards two large covered baskets which were standing in the shade. 'You do mean to go today, do you not? I was beginning to wonder, as you didn't come this morning.'

'I was prevented. We had a number of callers, and Mama was too tired to come down until noon.' Lucinda, to tell the truth, had forgotten that it was Wednesday, and her fortnightly visit to Cob End was due. 'I'd best set off now, or I'll be late back.'

'Can you manage both baskets?' Amy asked dubiously. 'I wish I could come with you, but Papa is adamant . . . I know, I'll come as far as the beginning of the Selvedge.'

Lucinda was relieved that she had Amy's company for the greater part of the walk, for the baskets were heavy, and the field path, after crossing the valley fields, rose steeply to the path which ran below the bottom terrace of the Pinnacles garden. It was the same route that she had taken with the cat Charlotte as far as that, and the rest of the way to Cob End was not much more than half a mile, on the level, running along the side of the ridge, at the very edge of the Forest. The two young ladies

chattered away about this and that on their way, stopping a couple of times to rest for a few minutes, for the
baskets were indeed heavy, and the day warm. Neither
mentioned the name of Mr Jones, and Mr Harris was
referred to only in connection with his invitation to ride
on Friday, which Amy was happy to accept.

The rest of their conversation might have surprised
anyone who thought young ladies had no interest in the
affairs of the world, for, after reporting on the local news
which she had gleaned during her visits about the town
that morning, Amy said, 'Papa was most upset this
morning. His newspaper came while we were at breakfast, and the news in it was very bad. It seems that
Bonaparte met with the Emperor of Russia a few days
ago, and they've signed a treaty!'

'Oh, heavens!' Lucinda exclaimed. 'Is it not amazing?
As fast as our government finds allies and forms a new
coalition, Bonaparte either defeats or suborns them! It's
little more than eighteen months since he beat the
Austrians and forced them to make a treaty with him,
and last autumn he trounced the Prussians, and now he's
beaten the Russians and turned them to his side. It
comes to stalemate every time, for he can't beat us at
sea, and we can't beat him on land!'

'I expect that now he will be threatening to invade us
again,' Amy observed pensively. 'I suppose that's why
so many soldiers have come to the camp here. The
number must have doubled in the past few days.'

'Has it?' Lucinda was startled. 'I hadn't realised . . .
But surely the barrack-blocks are full?'

'They've put up tents. It's only in the last two days,
and they came up the Navigation, in barges. You've
been too busy fighting fires and making jam to notice! I
asked Colonel Long why so many more men have come,
but he only tapped the side of his nose and winked. Now

there's a secretive man, if you like!'

'Quite rightly!' Lucinda exclaimed. 'Of course he shouldn't tell anyone what's happening just because they ask! Why, what if a spy happened to be listening . . .' Her voice tailed off as her mind put together what she had just said with Colonel Long's lost papers and their mysterious reappearance.

'What nonsense!' Amy failed to notice anything amiss. 'If a spy did happen to hear, how would he send the news to Bonaparte? I'm sure there's no postal service to France at present.'

Lucinda agreed, laughing, but there was still a tiny doubt in the back of her mind; someone had taken those papers, and then put them in the garden to be found . . .

The two friends fell silent as they toiled up the last steep field, for it was hot in the open, the sun blazing down as if August was bent on continuing the fine weather of July. At last they reached the place where they must part company, and both sat down on the grass for a final rest.

'The baby-clothes are for Mrs Smith,' Amy said, ticking items off on her fingers. 'The boots are for Mr Graygoose—they're old, but in good repair, and better than the ones he has. The knitted blanket is for old Mrs Howall, and the bull's-eyes are for the children, of course. You must give out the rest as you think fit. There's most of a leg of mutton, two fruit pies, some tea, sugar, jam and a bundle of stick beans, rhubarb, a couple of shirts, and the bread, of course.'

After a brief rest, Amy went back down the hill and Lucinda picked up the baskets and followed the Selvedge northwards, wondering, as she had often done before, about its name, for she could never make up her mind whether it was so called because it marked the edge of the Forest, or whether, indeed, the name referred to

the path or to the band of trees—hornbeams, mostly—
which bordered the Forest along its length.

About half-way between the bottom of the Pinnacles
garden and the thick hedge which marked the boundary
of the estate, the path forked, the lesser branch turning
up into the Forest to the source of a stream which flowed
down the hill on the Pinnacles side of the boundary
hedge. The main path continued past a great oak—or it
had done so until last night, for Lucinda found that the
tree had been struck by lightning in the storm, and only
part of its shattered trunk remained. To her surprise, it
was obvious that someone had been at work here, for the
wreckage had been cleared from the path, the fallen
branches were cut and stacked, the mess of leaves and
twigs gathered into a tidy pile, and part of one large
branch had been set against the bank above the path and
turned into a seat by adzing the top smooth and driving
stakes below it to hold it in position. Mr Harris was
sitting on it, surveying the view through a small telescope, and was so absorbed that he had failed to notice
Lucinda's approach. She stopped and looked at him,
and thought how cool and at ease he looked in a white
open-necked shirt, breeches and boots.

'Good afternoon, Mr Harris,' she said, at which he
started and almost dropped his telescope, but he recovered quickly, rose to his feet, bade her 'Good
afternoon' in his usual pleasant manner, and asked,
'Are you on your way to this mysterious Cob End of
yours?'

'Yes. Miss Martin usually comes with me, but her
father has forbidden her during this hot weather. I think
he fears she may take an infection,' Lucinda replied,
wondering if he would think her forward if she sat down
on his new seat for a few minutes, for the baskets had
become very heavy.

'The Rector has no similar fears for you, then?' Mr Harris enquired. He took her baskets from her, set them safely down in the shade, dusted the seat with his handkerchief, and gestured to her to sit, as she replied, 'He trusts in the Lord to protect me while I'm about his work,' then wished she had phrased it differently, and less like a prissy Methody-miss.

'Quite right!' Mr Harris sat beside her, stretching out his long booted legs and leaning back against the bank. 'What makes Cob End a likely source of infection? Are the people verminous, plague-ridden, or merely dirty?'

'They're short of water. All they have is a small stream, which they must use for drinking, washing and cooking. It comes from a weak spring, and dries up after a week without rain. Last night's storm will have helped a little, but the ground is so dry that it will soon soak away.'

'Why do they not dig wells?'

'Mr Marshall, their landlord, will not allow it.'

'How ridiculous! Why not?' Mr Harris shifted slightly, and his arm brushed against Lucinda's shoulder, setting a tingling sensation running through her, and she unobtrusively slid a few inches away from him, for they were too close for propriety.

'Well, really because he wishes to be rid of them. You see, all the people who live at Cob End used to work on the Forest House estate, but Mr Marshall pulled the house down when he bought the estate . . . but we've told you this before!'

'Yes. As I collect, he leases the valley land to the War Office, and shoots over the rest, and otherwise lets it go to rack and ruin.'

'That's right. The Cob-Enders were allowed to go on living in their cottages because they've nowhere else to go, but he charges them the full rent, and does no repairs, so the roofs are falling in and they're all in a bad state.'

'Why do they not leave, then?'

'Because they've nowhere else to go. They've no money, for there's no work for them on the Forest House estate any more, and if they start to work for someone else, Mr Marshall will evict them, for the cottages are tied, and then they'd have to go to the Poorhouse, as there are no cottages to let at a rent they could afford. There are so many extra men working at the powder-mill, because of the warm, that all the cottages in the district are let at quite high rents. They—the Cob-Enders, that is—can't go away, because they're too poor to hope to get settlement anywhere else—the churchwardens would simply send them back here—and a man can't up sticks and go away to look for work himself, leaving his wife and children on the parish.'

Mr Harris considered this information in silence for a while, and Lucinda deduced that he had been unaware of the drawbacks of the Poor Law arrangements, which required labouring people to gain a settlement certificate if they wished to move to a different place, but to be unable to do so unless they could prove that they would not become a charge on their new parish.

She sat looking at the view before her, which gave a wide prospect of the valley, from below the town to above the camp, with every detail of both clearly visible.

'How well you can see the camp from here,' she observed presently.

'Yes.' Mr Harris showed no great interest.

'I wonder—may I look through your telescope?' Lucinda asked hesitantly.

'By all means!' He handed her the instrument, and watched with an amused smile as she put it to her eye, but, of course, could not see anything but a blur of light. She lowered it, looked it over for a moment, then tried again, pulling it out slowly until the colourful splash of the flag flying over the camp sprang into view so clearly that she could make out the crosses on it. She followed the flagpole down and surveyed the rows of wooden barrack-huts, and then the ranks of tents beyond them. It appeared that the number of men in the camp must have doubled in the past two or three days, and she was about to comment on this, when something made her stop, consider, and decide not to mention it. It was an irrational decision, she realised as she made it, for Mr Harris had only to glance in that direction to see for himself, even without the telescope, and form his own conclusions.

'Have you found something of interest?'

'I was just looking across the valley. I've never had the opportunity to look through a telescope before.'

'You appear to be surveying the camp. All those colourful uniforms! There's nothing like a red coat to attract the ladies!' Mr Harris said with a slight edge to his voice. 'Will you oblige me by bending your gaze on the field next but one below us, and telling me what you see?'

Lucinda had to search about a little to find the field in question, for it was easy enough to see it with the naked eye, but much harder to locate in the small circle of the telescope.

'Yes, I see it now,' she said, and then a familiar figure entered her narrow field of vision. It was a man in a rusty black coat which had once belonged to her father, and a pair of green breeches with a large brown patch across the seat. There was a lurcher with him, and he was carrying a bundle of limp furry forms with long ears that hung down almost to the ground.

'And who is the fellow with the rabbits?' Mr Harris enquired.

Lucinda lowered the telescope, and turned a pale face and imploring eyes on him.

'If you take him before the magistrates,' she said, 'they will send him to prison, for he has no money to pay a fine. His wife and five children will either starve or go into the Poorhouse, and his neighbours will have no meat at all, apart from the odd scraps they're given out of charity. Are the rabbits so important to you? I doubt if he takes much above a dozen a week.'

'What's his trade?' Mr Harris's face was inscrutable.

'He's a handyman—a good one, who can turn his hand to most things. He was hedger and ditcher before . . .'

'There wouldn't happen to be a shepherd or a cowman at Cob End, I suppose?'

'Both,' Lucinda replied. 'But please—what do you mean to do about Mr W— . . . That man?'

'Rabbits,' said Mr Harris to the canopy of leaves above their heads, 'are not game within the meaning of the Game Laws. The most I could charge him with is trespass, and then only if he's done any damage. The trouble with rabbits'—transferring his gaze to Lucinda's anxious face—'is that they eat grass which should be consumed by sheep. In themselves, they form a useful source of food and fur, but they require strict control. What does Mr W— do with the skins?'

'His wife cures them,' she replied doubtfully, not sure whether his reply to her question implied that he did not intend to prosecute the poacher. 'She gave me a fur lining for my cloak last winter.'

'Why didn't she sell it to you?' His voice was sharp.

'Well—I suppose she wanted to give me something to . . . er . . . out of gratitude.'

'Because of all this?' He nudged the nearest basket

with his toe. 'What do you bring them?'

'Good cast-off clothes and boots, food—whatever we can collect.'

'We?'

'Amy—Miss Martin—and I.'

'I see. Would your Mr W— take regular work if he could get it?'

'He'd like to, but there's the problem of finding somewhere to live . . .'

'Mm.' Mr Harris was silent for a moment, then said, 'May I?' took back his telescope from Lucinda, and surveyed the landscape through it again.

'There's a vast amount of activity about the camp,' he said. 'I don't recollect seeing those tents before. Are there more men there than usual?'

'I believe so,' Lucinda replied reluctantly, again not sure why, for he could see that there were.

'I wonder why.' It sounded like a question, so Lucinda replied, 'I've no idea.'

'No rumours about the town? No confidential murmurs from the gallant Captain Bridges?'

'Captain Bridges,' she replied a shade tartly, 'is not given to confidential murmurs. He has more sense! Which reminds me—Miss Martin would be very happy to ride on Friday, if your invitation is still open.'

'By all means. I'm delighted!'

'But,' continued Lucinda, 'have you asked Captain Bridges yet?'

'No. I thought it best to ascertain first whether you and Miss Martin would come.'

'Then, if you wouldn't mind . . . I mean, if it's agreeable to you . . . Do you think you might ask Mr Jones instead?'

'Mr Jones? The Curate?' Mr Harris said blankly. 'If you wish. But I thought . . . It appeared to me that there was a certain—er—understanding between the Captain and Miss Martin.'

'Oh, that doesn't signify anything,' Lucinda assured him. 'Captain Bridges is attentive to Amy and me by turns, but not with any serious intent! He's a sensible and very dutiful young man, and will marry his family's choice in due course, and no doubt be perfectly happy. His connections wouldn't countenance a mere solicitor's daughter.'

'But Mr Jones?' The quizzical look on his face invited the sharing of confidences, but Lucinda, recollecting that the secret was not hers to share, merely replied, 'Mr Jones so rarely has a few hours of recreation, and both Miss Martin and I are very fond of him.'

'Are you, by Jove!' Mr Harris sounded the merest trifle miffed, and Lucinda wondered if she had offended him by more or less making him exchange Captain Bridges, who no doubt came from the same rank of Society as himself, for Mr Jones, who might seem to him a dull companion, being only a country curate. To make matters worse, she had to add a further request. 'The only thing is—he doesn't own a horse.'

'But he can ride, I suppose? In that case, another of my horses can take a little exercise. They're all in need of it.'

'Thank you very much,' she said hurriedly, before he could think of a reason why Mr Jones might not be invited. 'I must be on my way now, or I'll be late home.'

She rose, and went to pick up her baskets, but Mr Harris forestalled her, and said, 'I'll walk along with you and carry these. I've a mind to look at Cob End and its denizens, if you've no objection?'

Lucinda was, of course, pleased by the idea, although she told herself that her pleasure was due to the fact that, having seen the plight of the Cob-Enders, he would hardly be so hard-hearted as to prosecute Mr Warrener for trespass, and that walking along with him, alone, on such a fine afternoon, in such a lovely setting, had nothing to do with it.

They said very little, apart from observations on the various plants and birds that they saw, and neither commented on the hoof-marks which were sometimes visible in the softer parts of the path, some of them perhaps made by Captain Bridges's mount on one of his circular rides, but most of them too small—more pony-sized. Presently they came to the stream, which the path crossed on an old stone bridge, and to the stile in the thick, high quickset hedge on the boundary between Pinnacles and the Forest House estate.

Mr Harris swung himself and the baskets over the stile and handed Lucinda across, then, looking about him, observed, 'This is in an even worse state than my land! The path is almost overgrown, and the Forest seems to be full of dead wood.'

'Mr Marshall doesn't allow anyone to go into his part of the Forest, for fear they'll disturb his shooting.' The lack of expression in Lucinda's voice showed quite well what she thought of that gentleman. 'So the firewood, and the blackberries, the nuts and the puffballs are all ungathered, while the poor Cob-Enders, who could make good use of them . . .'

'Do their gathering in my part of the Forest.' Mr Harris finished for her, which was not what she had intended to say, although it was probably true.

The path twisted a little downhill, still following the edge of the Forest, then up again, and presently came to some ramshackle cottages on the far side of a deep-cut ditch containing a trickle of dubious-looking water.

'This is Cob End,' Lucinda said flatly.

Mr Harris made no reply, but stood looking at the

cottages with a frown deep enough to be called a scowl. He followed slowly as Lucinda negotiated the narrow plank bridge across the ditch, and set the baskets down on the ground as half a dozen children came out from behind the tumbledown fence of one of the cottages, where they had obviously been hiding.

'Mam!' shouted one of them. 'It's Miss Calvert and a strange gentleman!' The children clustered round Lucinda, replying shyly to her greetings and questions about their welfare, and shooting suspicious glances at the 'strange gentleman', who stood quietly in the background.

Presently a thin, anxious-looking woman in an old but carefully darned frock and a holland apron came out of the first cottage, wiping her hands on a piece of cloth, and welcomed Lucinda warmly enough, but looked at Mr Harris as if she feared he might bite. Lucinda introduced him, and told him that this was Mrs Warrener.

'Ah, the lady who cures rabbit-skins!' he said, much to Mrs Warrener's confusion and the girl's surprise.

'How did you know that?' Lucinda demanded. 'I made sure not to mention any names.'

'Don't you know what a warrener is?' he replied with some amusement. 'I've no doubt it's been the profession of this lady's husband's family for generations! May I speak with your husband, Mrs Warrener?'

The woman glanced nervously over her shoulder, then from side to side like a frightened animal, but made no reply.

'I wish to put a business proposition to him,' Mr Harris said gently. 'There'll be no trouble. On the contrary, what I have to say will be to his advantage.'

'Johnny, run and tell your dad,' the woman said to the largest of the children, but she still sounded frightened.

Mr Warrener appeared from the cottage after a few

moments, looking sidelong and suspiciously at Mr Harris, but wiped his hand on the side of the green breeches and accepted that gentleman's proffered handshake.

'There are too many rabbits on my land,' Mr Harris said briskly. 'They need to be farmed, if you understand me. Not wiped out, but kept within reasonable limits as they were in the past, probably by your forebears? I understand that you can't officially be employed by me at present, or you'll lose your cottage, so I suggest that, for the time being, you carry on as you have been doing, but take the coneys in somewhat greater numbers, as you think fit, and sell the surplus, and also the skins, of course. You know how to go about doing the job, I take it?'

Mr Warrener gazed open-mouthed for a second, but he was far from unintelligent, and once the first shock had worn off, a beatific smile appeared on his face, and he said, 'Ay, I do that, mester! You're not going to plough the warren, then?'

'No. I mean to keep sheep and cows, and the only crops will be for fodder. Turnips, clover and so forth, which will do better on the lower land. You may have noticed that I'm building over by the road, near my lodge. There'll be decent cottages there for two cow-men, two shepherds, a general handyman and, of course, a warrener-*cum*-hedger, when they're finished. If you know anyone who would be good at the work, and would like to apply, I'll be pleased to interview them. I want no shirkers and no ignoramuses, mind you! They'll need to know the work, and do it well, or they'll not stay in my employ.'

Mr Warrener looked at his wife, who was staring, transfixed, at Mr Harris, as if he had suddenly turned into a golden angel in front of her eyes. 'Ay, mester!' he exclaimed. 'I know just the men for you, and they'll be that grateful, they'll work themselves to the bone, you'll see!'

'Don't you want to know about the wages?' Mr Harris's smile, never far from those thin lips, broadened considerably. 'I gather that ten shillings a week is the going rate hereabouts.'

'And—And the rent, sir?' Mrs Warrener spoke hoarsely, but had at last found her voice.

'The same as you're paying here. You can find your own firewood and other pickings in my tract of the Forest, and there'll be some bags of good seed for the gardens, and a piglet to fatten for Christmas every year.' Mr Harris still spoke briskly, as if to finish what he had to say before his hearers died of shock. 'Meanwhile, as I gather you're also a hedger and ditcher, and the cottages won't be ready for a while yet, I suggest that you cut a hole in my boundary hedge at the nearest point and put in a gate—you can collect the wood from the yard up at the house. There's a good flow of water in the stream just beyond the hedge, and I don't suppose you'll mind carrying it for a few weeks until you move. I take it you're willing to accept my offer?'

Mr Warrener's reply was hardly coherent, but the gist of it was clearly enough in the affirmative, and the news spread quickly to the other Cob-Enders, who had been lurking in the background, wondering what the strange gentleman wanted with Bill Warrener. They were all thrown into such a state of euphoria, once the meaning of it all had penetrated, that the distribution of Lucinda's gifts was almost an anticlimax.

Mr Harris seemed disinclined to bask in his glory, but went with Mr Warrener to seek a good place to pierce the hedge, and then returned and fidgeted about in the background, fending off grateful Cob-Enders while

Lucinda finished giving out food, clothing and advice. She did not linger afterwards, for it was really getting late, but said goodbye quickly, collected her empty baskets, and indicated to him that she was ready to leave.

'It's very good of you,' she began as they crossed his gushing stream, so different from the dirty trickle at Cob End, but he interrupted with, 'Oh, pray don't start. It's all quite as much to my advantage as it is to theirs! I don't offer work out of charity, but only after careful enquiries about the fitness of the prospective employee for the job. Tell me, what is being done about the fire-engine? I collect that the old one is beyond repair.'

'Oh, quite, for it was burnt as well as crushed. Father and Mr Jones are gone to London to order another.'

'And how is it to be paid for?'

Lucinda repeated her father's remark about the deep-pocketed ravens, at which Mr Harris laughed and requested her to tell the Rector he might be put down for ten guineas. But once again he rejected her attempts to thank him, and talked resolutely of sheep, cows, rabbits, deer and wild birds, while Lucinda strolled along with him, basking in the pleasure of his company, with a slightly guilty feeling of gratitude to Mr Martin for preventing Amy from coming with her, which had resulted in this most enjoyable opportunity to talk to Mr Harris—or, rather, to listen to him, for there was little need for her to say anything at all.

She could not help recollecting Amy's words, and realised that this was one of those golden moments to gloat over which her friend had mentioned, and yet . . . There was nothing of himself in his discourse, no clue to anything about him except an enthusiasm for animals, domesticated or wild, which, by his own admission, was quite recent in origin.

'Were you brought up in the country?' She hoped that the question sounded as if it had arisen naturally from his conversation.

'No. Most of my childhood was spent abroad, or at school, and then at university. I've always looked out from coach windows at the countryside, and wished . . . I've read a great deal, but it's not the same.'

'You've never been to France, though? Is it not difficult to go abroad without entering France?'

'I didn't say I had never been to France,' he replied, his ironic smile twisting his lips. 'It was Paris, if you recollect. There's a great deal more of a country than its capital city. In any case, one may travel in a number of different directions about the world without entering France at all, you know!'

'I suppose so,' Lucinda replied blankly, wondering how anyone could answer in so courteous a fashion and yet be completely evasive, for she was none the wiser about his foreign travels than she had been an hour ago.

'May I take up a little more of your time to show you how the new cottages are coming along?' he asked. 'I'll send you home in my carriage, of course.'

'I—I think it would be better not,' Lucinda said reluctantly. 'To go home in your carraige, I mean. Tongues wag in a small town, you know. Once might escape remark, but not twice in less than a se'nnight! Thank you for the offer, though, and I have time to see the cottages and still be home in good time for dinner. I should very much like to see them.' She was agreeably flattered by the invitation.

There was much activity about the site where the cottages were being built, and the appearance of their employer seemed to stir the builders to a positive frenzy, mixing mortar like men possessed, and almost running with their hods of bricks.

'Brick-built cottages are not yet common hereabouts,' Lucinda observed. 'I suppose there'll be more of them, now that bricks are becoming cheaper.'

'Lath and plaster mostly, I suppose?' Mr Harris said. 'All very well, but it don't last like brick. I think this first one stands high enough to give an idea of what I have in mind.' He ushered Lucinda into what was in fact the bottom half of a cottage, with its walls standing about five feet high.

'Proper foundations,' he said, 'and a large kitchen, which will have an iron kitchener built into the fireplace, and a brick oven, so the women can bake. I think it ridiculous that so many of the labouring class have to buy poor quality bread for the lack of a means to bake their own. This is the scullery, where there'll be a copper with a firebox below it, and a stone sink with a small handpump—there's adequate water about fifteen feet down, so each cottage will have its own well. The other two rooms, as you see, are not large, but enough for a couple and three or four children. If they feel a need for more rooms, they can put in a little attic, or build a lean-to for themselves. The garden should be large enough to grow a selection of vegetables, and there'll be a brick pigsty at the end of the garden, next the privy. I think your Cob-Enders will find it better than their present hovels!'

'They'll think it's Paradise!' Lucinda exclaimed, looking about her in amazement. 'Are you really not going to charge more rent than they're paying now? It's only a shilling a week, you know.'

'It'll pay for most of the upkeep. I wondered about washing-lines. Perhaps you could advise me, for I know little of such things? I thought a stout pole in the fence at each side of the garden would be in order, but should there be another in the middle? I can't work out how one prevents the weight of the wet washing from causing it to dip in the middle and trail in the mud across such a width.'

'One has a clothes-prop,' Lucinda confided. 'It lifts up the line wherever needed.'

'Ah!' exclaimed the enlightened Mr Harris. 'Now, if you think of anything which I've overlooked, you will inform me, I hope?'

'I'm sure you haven't overlooked anything.' Lucinda looked about her, thinking how lucky the Cob-Enders were to be after all their misfortunes. 'If I do think of anything, I'll be sure to mention it. Now, if you'll excuse me, Gabriel struck five just now, and I must go if I'm not to be late.'

Mr Harris walked with her as far as the point where her path struck off down the hill, and stood looking after her as she half-ran down the slope, and she turned at the first field-gate to wave to him, which he acknowledged with an uplifted hand before turning homewards.

Lucinda continued on her way, thinking happily how good and kind he was, how handsome, how pleasant to be with, and all the other thoughts which might be expected from a young lady in the first delicious stages of falling in love. There was, nevertheless, still that one shadow over her happiness—the continued evasiveness of the gentleman, for she could hardly doubt that he was deliberately avoiding giving any information about his background.

She was not particularly surprised to encounter Monsieur Roland in the third field through which she passed, for he was given to taking solitary walks about the countryside, neither was she surprised that he was seated on the log on which she often rested herself, scribbling away in a notebook, for his landlady had once told her that he spent much of his time writing. She had never, of course, questioned him about it, or even mentioned it, but she sometimes wondered if he wrote books, or perhaps articles for a journal or magazine, under an assumed name. If he did, it would account for his good clothes and apparent sufficiency of income, which was obviously more than he could earn by his French lessons.

She called a greeting as she approached him, and he looked up, startled, then rose to his feet, putting his book away in his pocket. He made no mention of what he had been doing, but enquired, seeing the baskets, if she had been visiting the poor unfortunates at Cob End.

'Yes, I have, and oh, Monsieur Roland! Such good news! Mr Harris is going to employ them, and give them new brick cottages to live in. They can hardly believe their good fortune, after the misery they've been in for so long.'

'Indeed!' He raised his eyebrows, but seemed less enthusiastic than she expected, so she told him in more detail as they walked along, he now carrying the baskets, about the offer of access to Mr Harris's stream, and the promise of work, and then about the cottages with all their built-in conveniences.

'And he's even thought about washing-lines!' she concluded.

'*Comment?*' he enquired, looking puzzled. 'Oh, ropes for the wet clothes—I understand. Well, it is all to 'is advantage, of course! 'E puts these people under great obligation to 'im, and then 'e can make them work very 'ard. Then, also, if the cottages are so comfortable and convenient, they will not wish to leave them for something worse. Oh, 'e is very clever, your Mr 'Arris! 'E gets the acclaim and the gratitude due to a great benefactor, and good, faithful labourers into the bargain!'

'I'm sure he doesn't think of it in that way at all!' Lucinda felt quite indignant.

'Does 'e not? 'Ow can you be sure? What do you know of the man? To be sure, 'e seems attractive and rich—it is very easy to be kind if one is so rich that a few 'undred pounds 'ere or there is of no matter. For me, I do not trust 'im! I know that I saw 'im in Paris, yet 'e says 'e was never there. If a man is false in one thing, 'e is likely to be false in all things, in my experience.' His French accent had become much more pronounced in his agitation.

'But are you sure that you saw him?' Lucinda protested. 'It was what—five years ago? And only for a few moments? You could be mistaken!'

'Nevair!' Monsieur Roland declared with Gallic emphasis. 'I do not forget a face, particularly one coming from the 'ouse of that—that *scélérat*! It was 'e, I tell you. 'E who calls 'imself John 'Arris.'

CHAPTER SEVEN

On HER return home, Lucinda found that Fred, in a fit of misguided kindness, had presented a deceased rodent to Miss Enston, and was now being excessively miffed half-way up the walnut tree, while the lady was lying on Mrs Calvert's sofa upstairs, clutching a smelling-bottle and recovering from a fit of strong hysterics. The Rector and Mr Jones had returned exhausted from their foray into the Great Metropolis and were reviving themselves with a glass of sherry or two in the garden, discreetly withdrawn to two chairs on the far side of the mulberry tree. There Lucinda joined them, being too depressed by Monsieur Roland's strictures on Mr Harris to feel up to dealing with Miss Enston.

She could not help, however, being cheered by the news that Mr Calvert had discovered at the insurance company that the Churchwardens had, by some extraordinary piece of foresight, insured the old fire-engine against destruction by fire for the cost of replacing it, and that the company, prudently realising that another fire in the town in the absence of an engine could be very expensive for them, had advanced the money at once. This had emboldened the two clergymen to bespeak a larger and more efficient model, trusting that they would be able to raise the extra money before the new engine was delivered the following week.

'Mr Harris says you may put him down for ten guineas,' Lucinda said.

'Mr Harris? Have you seen him today, then?' the Rector asked.

'I encountered him on the way to Cob End. And, Father, he has offered employment to the people there, and the new cottages he's building—by the lodge, you remember?—they are for them! Is it not good news?'

Both the Rector and Mr Jones were as pleased as Lucinda, and she found comfort in the fact that neither cast any doubts about Mr Harris's motives. There was further good news for her, for after dinner, when Miss Enston and Fred had both been mollified and had parted amicably, and Mr Jones had gone off to his lonely and not very comfortable lodgings, Mr Calvert produced a parcel apiece for his wife and daughter.

'I had time to call at the Royal Exchange to make some purchases,' he explained, 'and I thought you might both like a little frippery.'

His wife's gift was a pretty Indian shawl, which was rather in the nature of coals to Newcastle, as she had at least a dozen already, but it was nevertheless welcome, for it was a vital article of fashion, and a lady could no more manage without yet another new shawl than she could without at least as many bonnets. Mrs Calvert, after a few minor criticisms, was pleased to approve it, and even said that she would wear it for church on Sunday, if she felt well enough to attend.

With that settled, attention turned to Lucinda's parcel, which proved to contain a length of green poplin for a new evening gown.

'I noticed that your best gown was quite ruined by the fire,' her father explained with modest pride. 'I wasn't sure about the colour, but you usually wear green, and I like you in it, and Mr Jones supported my feeling that it would be becoming to you. I do hope it will suit . . .'

'Mr Jones, indeed!' Mrs Calvert, had she not been a lady, might be said to have snorted. 'And, pray, what does Mr Jones know of such matters?'

'He has good eye for colour, my dear, and is of an age to notice what is becoming to a young lady,' the Rector replied firmly, for there was limit to what he would tolerate from his wife.

'It's very pretty, Father, and I do like green,' Lucinda said, kissing him. 'Thank you very much. It was most kind of you to think of it!'

There had, of course, to be much discussion between mother and daughter on the design of the new gown, but this was settled to their mutual satisfaction, and it was decided that Lucinda should take the length to the dressmaker first thing in the morning, for undoubtedly either Mr Martin or the Longs would soon be giving a dinner-party to return Mr Harris's hospitality.

Lucinda went to bed happy enough that night, but woke in the small hours with the feeling that a strange noise had disturbed her rest. She lay still for a few moments, listening, then heard an odd sound from the garden, below her open window.

She had a good idea what it might be, but slipped out of bed and cautiously put her head out of the window to be sure. She saw two dark figures below, carrying something fairly small and heavy, which was carefully placed under the hanging ivy near the kitchen door. The two figures then returned to the garden gate and disappeared into the night, with only the faintest sound of hooves on the roadway, as if the ponies' feet were muffled.

As nothing unusual had occurred, Lucinda returned to bed without a second thought about the matter, but found herself unable to get to sleep again. She lay awake for an hour or more, piecing together what she knew of

Mr Harris and trying to make sense of it, but could conclude only that he had given away precious little about himself, and the tremulous feeling which ran through her at the very thought of him was quite unjustified, for he might well be the blackest of wolves in sheep's clothing for all she knew.

It was a very dispiriting conclusion, for she could not doubt, after being with him for a couple of hours that afternoon, that he had a powerfully disturbing effect on her, and, to judge from Amy's description of the state of being in love, the diagnosis of her own ailment was clear. It did not by any means fill her with joy, and she shed a few tears over it before she eventually fell asleep.

The visit to the dressmaker took up the greater part of the morning, but Lucinda had just time before luncheon to call on Amy and return the baskets and to tell her all the latest news, not least that concerning the Cob-Enders, and also that the riding expedition was arranged for the next afternoon. But she did not mention that Mr Jones was to be of the party, in case he was unable to accept the invitation.

She need not have worried, however, for Mr Harris arrived at the Rectory after luncheon on Friday with five horses, a groom, and Mr Jones, whom he had collected on his way. Amy was already at the Rectory with Lucinda, so the party was able to set off almost at once.

At Mr Harris's request, they went first along the Navigation, which ran beside the river but pursued a straight course, while the river meandered about, sometimes a quarter-mile from the Navigation, and sometimes divided from it only by a bank. They rode on the track provided for the convenience of barge-horses, which was wide enough for two to ride abreast. Mr Harris rode with Amy, Lucinda followed with Mr Jones, and the groom ambled along behind, chewing a straw and staring morosely between his mount's ears.

The leading couple were soon engaged in lively chatter, but Lucinda found Mr Jones unusually heavy going, which surprised her, for he was usually a good conversationalist. He answered quite briefly when necessary, but otherwise maintained a gloomy absence of mind, looking straight ahead without so much as a glance at the attractions of river and meadow.

After a while, when they had passed the army camp, which was clearly visible from the riverside at a distance of half a mile across the fields, just above the flood-plain level, a branching bridle-path struck off eastwards, and Amy, to judge from her gestures, seemed inclined to follow it.

As the others caught up, she turned and said, 'Shall we go this way? It's a pleasant path, and one of my favourites.'

'By all means,' Lucinda replied, 'for it goes up into the Forest eventually, and the views are fine.' The gentlemen were agreeable, so they turned away from the river and set off across the fields.

Somehow, in the change of direction, places were also changed. Mr Jones moved forward to take the lead with Amy, and Mr Harris dropped back alongside Lucinda.

'Your friend is a witty and intelligent young lady,' he commented quietly to Lucinda. 'But I think she might prefer things as they are now, rather than as they were!'

'Yes.' She was pleased that he was so perceptive, and even more pleased to be riding with him, yet suddenly bereft of anything to say. This did not seem to worry Mr Harris, who looked about him and commented on the beauties of nature, the progress of the crops in the fields, and whatever else caught his eye.

Their route took them along the northern edge of the

camp, which was fairly seething with activity, but he did not make any remark on that, only slowing his horse a little and looking keenly about at what was going on.

'I've never seen so many men there before,' Lucinda observed. 'I hope this doesn't mean that the French may be about to invade, after all!'

'Not unless they've learned to fly!' Mr Harris replied cheerfully.

'There was talk of balloons . . .'

'So there was, but the wind tends to blow the wrong way. They would probably end up in the German States if they tried that!'

As they went from one field to another, it was, of course, necessary to open and shut gates. Mr Jones did the opening, usually by leaning down and using the stock of his crop to unhook the wire or string loop which held gate to post, and the groom dismounted to close and fasten them. He was a lugubrious-looking fellow, who did not seem to enjoy jogging along gently about the countryside.

At the second field beyond the camp, they came upon Monsieur Roland, perched on top of a gate, writing in his notebook. He slid to the ground as they approached, greeted Mr Jones and Miss Martin in a friendly manner, and opened the gate for them. Then he said, 'Good afternoon, Miss Calvert,' and ignored Mr Harris altogether.

'Good afternoon, Monsieur Roland,' Lucinda replied. 'Do you not remember Mr Harris?'

'Yes, very well!' he replied with meaning, and bowed coldly, at which Mr Harris smiled broadly and said, 'A pleasant afternoon for a walk!' in French. There was no reply, but he busied himself in shutting the gate, apparently not noticing the groom, who uttered an indignant, 'Oi! If you *don't* mind, sir!'

Monsieur Roland said something vaguely apologetic and let the groom through, then shut the gate and stood staring after the riders over the top of it. Lucinda turned to wave to him, and he raised his demi-bateau in response.

'I'm afraid he's still convinced that he saw you in Paris,' Lucinda said apologetically to Mr Harris. 'He has a very deep hatred of the present government of France, of course, and of the Revolution, for it robbed him of everything.'

'Has he no family?'

'No one in England. I don't know about France; he's never mentioned anyone.'

'What are his circumstances?'

'I've no idea. He doesn't volunteer much about his affairs, and one doesn't wish to appear prying . . .' Lucinda suddenly recollected that Mr Harris was not inclined to volunteer much either, and felt her colour rise. Mr Harris noted this, and remarked, 'Secretive lot of men about here, ain't there?' at which Lucinda blushed even more.

Harvesting had started in many of the cornfields, and the riders stopped to watch the work. Mr Harris plucked a trail of honeysuckle from the hedgerow, twined it into a wreath, and presented it to Lucinda, saying, 'Would you like a trimming for your hat?'

It was a small sorrow with Lucinda that she could not match Amy's smart riding-habit, which was dark blue and very dashing with military-style frogging and a feminine version of a Hussar's busby. She had to be content with an old one of her mother's, altered to fit, in a dull grey, which she had endeavoured to improve with green braid, and a hat with a curly brim and a shallow crown, which she had contrived out of an old clerical hat of her father's, covered with a left-over piece of the grey fabric and trimmed with a couple of pheasant feathers. The honeysuckle looked slightly absurd on it, but she wore it nevertheless, wondering privately whether Mr Harris had been making fun of her garb, or had meant the gift kindly.

The ground began to rise beyond the cornfield, and the path became more meandering to lessen the steepness of the climb. From time to time the riders paused to look back down the hill or across the valley, drawing Mr Harris's attention to various things of interest. Eventually they reached the edge of the Forest, and here Mr Harris proposed that they might rest and take refreshment.

His companions were mystified about the latter part of his proposal, for they had not noticed the saddlebags on the groom's mount, but as soon as they had dismounted and tethered the horses, the bags were unpacked, and an interesting variety of sandwiches, cakes and bottles of lemonade were set out on a white cloth spread on the grass. It was very pleasant, sitting on the grass, eating and drinking and looking down on the little world below them in the valley. The food was delicious, for the sandwiches contained ham, lobster, a peppery relish and cucumber, and the cakes were light sponges decorated with sugar icing. There was also a basin of little wild strawberries, which had been covered with a cloth and wedged upright in the corner of a saddlebag.

'I regret that there's no cream,' Mr Harris said as Lucinda spooned the berries into the dishes provided, 'but I could not contrive to keep it fresh and unspilled. The Cob End children brought me the fruit this morning, in a selection of cabbage-leaves. They must have been out since dawn to find so many! I suggested they should sit down and help me to eat them, but young Master Warrener, who seems to be their gaffer, insisted that they were all for me, and I'd no wish to offend them, so we had cakes instead.'

'They appreciate what you're doing for them,' Lucinda said.

Mr Jones was anxious to hear what Mr Harris was planning to do, both with the Cob-Enders and with his land, and both gentlemen were soon deep in conversation, so presently Amy and Lucinda wandered away a little, and stood looking down on the town.

'Whatever is that?' Amy asked, pointing. 'Look, on the Navigation—do you see? Why, it looks for all the world like a giant sea-serpent!'

Lucinda, who was a trifle long-sighted, could make out what it was rather better than Amy, and replied, 'It's a string of barges, but I've never seen so many on the river. There must be a hundred! Whatever can they be doing?'

'They're going to the powder-mill!' Amy exclaimed. 'The leaders have turned into the mill cut, and the mill grounds look like an ant-heap. I do wish we could see better.'

Lucinda, on a sudden impulse, turned and called, 'Mr Harris! Do you happen to have your telescope with you?'

The gentlemen looked up in surprise, and came to see what was attracting the ladies' attention, Mr Harris pulling his little telescope from his pocket as he came. He gave it to Lucinda, who extended it and focused in a business-like manner, while Amy pointed out the activity at the mill and the procession of barges on the Navigation.

'Oh!' exclaimed Lucinda, as the area within the circle of the telescope suddenly sprang to life. 'It's the rockets!'

Mr Harris suddenly took the telescope from her as she

turned her head away from it to tell the others what she had seen, and put it to his eye. 'Yes, indeed. Things are moving!' And he added, almost under his breath, so that only Lucinda heard, 'They'll be in time, after all!'

'In time for what?' she asked, but Mr Jones, in a puzzled tone, enquired, 'Rockets? What rockets? Do they make fireworks at the powder-mill, then? I thought it was all powder for cannon.'

Lucinda hesitated, not sure to what extent the development of Colonel Congreve's invention was supposed to be a secret, but Mr Harris replied, 'Did you never hear of the problems the army in India had in '99, when Tippu Sultan used explosive rockets against them at Seringapatam? The son of the Comptroller of Woolwich Arsenal has invented an improved variety for our artillerymen, which was used to good effect against the French camps at Boulogne last year.'

'Rockets, though?' Mr Jones seemed even more puzzled. 'Little cylinders of pasteboard, with a pinch of powder in each and a long stick? What use are they in war, except perhaps for signalling?'

'Imagine one this size'—Mr Harris held out his hands before him—'made of metal, packed with gunpowder, and weighing forty, or even sixty pounds, with a six-foot stick . . . Not exactly a firework, eh?'

Mr Jones seemed to find the idea difficult to grasp, and Amy said, 'I don't know what use they'd be, except to make a very loud bang.'

Mr Harris looked at her with a somewhat bleak expression, but did not enlighten her about the damage that such a missile could do to a close formation of infantry soldiers, and then he turned to Lucinda, whose face told him that she had more imagination than her friend.

'I don't think we should talk about them too much,'

she said hesitantly. 'None of the men who work at the mill ever mentions them, and neither does Colonel Long or Captain Bridges.'

'You think Bonaparte's ears are long enough to hear us?' Mr Harris enquired, giving her a sharper look than the jocular words warranted.

'I suppose he has spies,' she replied. It was not an idea that she had ever put into words before, even to herself, but she had always been reluctant to speak to anyone about the odd scraps of information which came her way about the doings at the mill or the camp.

As she spoke, she looked at Mr Harris, straight in the face. His eyes met hers and held them for one long look, and then he turned away, gazing down towards the town, and said, 'I stand corrected. Shall we resume our ride?'

'I—I didn't mean . . .' Lucinda began.

'No, of course not,' he replied agreeably. 'Nevertheless, it looks to me as if there's a ride of some sort running among the trees, continuing our bridle-path.'

Lucinda looked in the direction he indicated. 'Yes, at least, there used to be, but we're on Mr Marshall's land, so it may be rather overgrown.'

'Shall we try it?' Mr Harris put his hand under her elbow and guided her back towards the horses, following Amy and Mr Jones, who were walking along with their heads a little closer together than was altogether proper. 'Speaking of Mr Marshall, I'm engaged to visit him tomorrow, to discuss the Cob-Enders.'

'Is he going to evict them?' Lucinda stopped in her tracks at the awful thought, and Mr Harris, caught unawares, swung towards her so that he knocked her off balance, and caught her in his arms to prevent her from falling over.

Lucinda shivered at the sudden close contact with

him, and her body instinctively stiffened, so that, sens-
ing it, he looked at her in surprise and exclaimed, 'I'm
very sorry! I wasn't expecting you to stop so suddenly!
Have I alarmed you?'

'No—at least, only about the Cob-Enders!' Lucinda
assured him quickly, beginning to walk on. 'If he evicts
them now, where are they to go? Your cottages won't be
ready for weeks yet.'

'Their situation is unchanged,' he replied, falling into
step beside her. 'I mean to talk to him about my plans,
and if the atmosphere seems favourable, ask him to let
them stay at Cob End, yet work for me, until the
cottages are finished. He may well agree, if he realises
that he'll be rid of them all the sooner by obliging me. If
he refuses, I shall not employ them until the cottages are
ready, and he'll have no grounds for evicting them. I'll
be very careful, have no fear.'

'You're very kind,' Lucinda said gratefully, for the
fate of the poor folk at Cob End had been of great
concern to her for a long time.

'It's all to my eventual advantage! I've talked with all
the men now, and found them most satisfactory. They
know their work, and they're obviously only too anxious
to resume their old occupations. Besides, the children
bring me rare treasures.'

The woodland ride proved to be passable, although
overgrown to some extent by bushes and saplings, and it
was cool and pleasant among the trees, and very peaceful, for there was no sound except the sleepy chirping of
a few birds, torpid in the afternoon heat, the faint stir of
the leaves, and the occasional crack or rustle which add
to the mystery of a forest.

It was past six when Lucinda reached home, and her
parents were already at dinner. Mr Harris called in for a
few minutes to apologise for bringing her back so late,

and stayed to take a glass of claret with the Rector, but politely declined the offer of a place at table, saying that he was expected at home.

When he had gone, and Lucinda had eaten her meat, Mrs Calvert rang for the pudding, having delayed its serving until her daughter caught up, and said, 'I do think you might give a little more thought before you go gallivanting off for hours at a time! I particularly wished you to visit Mrs Long this afternoon.'

'I'm sorry, Mama, but you made no mention of it at luncheon, and you knew that Amy and I were going riding.'

'I didn't know about Mrs Long at luncheon,' Mrs Calvert said airily. 'The news reached me at four, when Colonel Long called to tell me that his wife was unwell.'

'I'm sorry to hear it,' Lucinda said sincerely. 'Did he tell you what is the matter?'

'He did.' Mrs Calvert gave the Rector a hard look, and he, after a moment of puzzlement, said, 'I'll just er . . .' rose, and went out into the garden, where he wandered about aimlessly.

'It appears,' Mrs Calvert whispered portentously, leaning closer to her daughter, 'that Mrs Long is in expectation again, and is always given to bouts of not feeling quite the thing in the early weeks. She has a great desire for mulberries. You understand me?'

'Yes, Mama,' Lucinda replied with a commendably straight face. 'I'll take her a dish of them first thing in the morning. Shall I call Father, for here comes Annie with the pudding?'

Mr Calvert, on his return, was curious to know where the young ladies had taken Mr Harris on their expedition, and it took Lucinda some time to tell him all they had seen, omitting any mention of the activity at the powder-mill, but she found time, before sunset, to go into the church to see if a clean altar-cloth would be needed for Sunday.

It was very quiet and dark in the great building, for the Norman windows were small and the walls very thick, and the fact that the church had a western tower meant that there was no great west window to light that end of the nave, only a small one at the end of the south aisle, through which a blaze of golden light illuminated a small area, leaving the rest of the interior all the more shadowy in contrast. Consequently it was not until Lucinda reached the chancel that she realised that anyone else was in the church. Mr Jones was sitting in his usual place, not praying or reading, but immobile, staring straight before him.

'Mr Jones?' Lucinda said tentatively. 'Are you not well?'

He roused himself with a start and stood up, turning a mournful face towards her in the dim light. 'Quite well, thank you, Miss Calvert. I was thinking.'

'Is something troubling you?' she asked. 'Have you had bad news?'

'No, nothing of that sort.' She had never before heard him sound so sad.

'But you seemed so happy this afternoon. Was—Was Miss Martin . . . unkind to you?' It was not quite the word she wanted, for she could not imagine Amy ever being deliberately unkind to anyone.

'Not in the least!' he replied quickly, and then, realising what her question implied, sank down in his seat again and said wretchedly, 'Are my feelings so obvious? Am I the laughing-stock of the whole parish?'

Lucinda sat down at the end of the bench and said soothingly, 'Of course not! I doubt if anyone else has noticed anything at all. What *is* the matter? I thought you were both getting along famously during our ride.'

'We were,' he sighed. 'But it came over me, while I was savouring the memory of it, how kind she is, and how hopeless my—my case. I'm not good enough for her!'

'Not good enough!' Lucinda exclaimed, then, realising where she was, moderated her voice and went on, 'Whatever do you mean?'

'Just that. She's so beautiful, kind, good, so accomplished. Everyone admires her, and her family will, quite properly, wish her to make a good marriage! How can I, a humble curate, aspire to . . . Oh, it's hopeless!'

Lucinda thought for a moment, and then enquired with apparent inconsequence, 'What made you take Holy Orders?'

'I was called,' he replied simply.

'You're sure? It wasn't just something that you'd always wanted?'

'No, far from it! I fought against it for years, for my ambitions were far more worldly, but the Lord wanted me for His service and I had eventually to surrender. I've not regretted it, of course.'

'But surely,' Lucinda carefully kept her voice free of the triumph she felt that he had allowed her to manoeuvre him into exactly the answer she required, 'if God thinks you are good enough for His service, it's quite illogical to claim that you are not good enough for Amy Martin? You don't really believe that her requirements are higher than His, do you?'

Mr Jones opened his mouth, but was unable to find an answer, so he shut it again, thought for a few moments, and then said, 'But she was only being kind, and her father would wish someone better. I mean . . .'

'Amy was not being kind!' Lucinda assured him. 'She's not such a fool as to encourage a gentleman out of a mistaken sense of compassion. I'll admit that Mr

Martin would wish her to marry a man of reasonable fortune, but he would certainly consider her happiness more important than wealth!'

'Oh, money's no problem,' Mr Jones said quite blithely, suddenly appearing much more cheerful. 'I've a private income, and I come into another two thousand a year when I marry, from a trust fund. Do you think she . . . er . . .?'

'Yes,' she replied positively. 'Why don't you go and ask her?'

'Dare I? Shall I? Yes, I shall!' Mr Jones progressed from doubt to confidence in seven words, and sprang to his feet. 'At least, I'll seek an interview with Mr Martin now! Immediately! Thank you, Miss Lucinda! Good night!' And with that, he strode down the nave in a resolute fashion, then stopped by the last pew to turn to face the altar and kneel in prayer for a few seconds. He rose and went out, opening the door on a sunset glow which turned him briefly to a silhouette against the outer door of the porch, and then the door closed and the church was left darker than ever.

Lucinda, wishing him well, prayed for a while for him and for Amy, but then her thoughts and prayers turned to herself and Mr Harris. She no longer had any doubts about her feelings for him, and even just thinking about him gave her a curious melting feeling inside, but it was now becoming important to her to form some idea of his feelings for her, if any, and on that she could form no opinion at all.

Certainly, he seemed to enjoy her company, but she was well aware that she was reasonably attractive in appearance, a good listener and a not unintelligent conversationalist, and a great many other people could equally be said to enjoy her company and welcome her presence without in the least being in the state of mind

and heart towards her which she could wish for in Mr
Harris. She had to admit that she could not, by any
stretch of imagination, claim to have detected any signs
in his manner towards her to indicate that her wishes
were likely to be granted!

If only he were not so reserved! He was affable and
pleasant on the surface, and not in the least haughty or
distant, yet any attempt to penetrate beneath that surface made no progress at all. It was not precisely like
coming against a brick wall, but she was reminded of the
old schoolroom story about Richard Coeur de Lion,
when Richard laughed at the frail lightness of Saladin's
Saracen sword, set against the heavy solid iron of his
own, until Saladin challenged him to cut a cushion with
it . . . She could understand how Richard must have felt
as the cushion gently absorbed his blade, yet remained
unpenetrated. Mr Harris was like that cushion, but
where could she find the sharp scimitar . . .?

But what would she find inside if she ever did pierce
his armour? Why was he so reluctant to talk about his
past? Why was Monsieur Roland so certain that he was
lying about never having been in Paris? Surely, if Mr
Harris was the man he had seen, there could be no harm
in admitting it? There were any number of good reasons
why a foreigner in France might call at the house of the
French Foreign Minister, so why deny it?

Possibly Monsieur Roland was mistaken, yet it was
true that he had an excellent memory for anything or
anyone he had seen. He had once described Louis XVI
and Marie Antoinette to Amy and herself in a way that
brought their appearance so clearly to mind that the two
young ladies had only to close their eyes to visualise the
unfortunate king and queen! She could not really believe
that he would be so positive if he had any doubt at all.
Neither could she imagine that he would lie about such

an unimportant matter. She had always found him a scrupulous man, who would not lightly impugn another's character, yet he had openly called Mr Harris a liar! She could think of no reason at all why he should do that unless he was certain.

Admittedly, she liked the Frenchman, so would not wish to think ill of him. It was very sad that he had been forced to leave his country by the Revolution, fleeing in fear of his life, losing everything—family, home, fortune—and to spend so many long years in exile, without even the comfort of someone else to speak to in his own language, for the only French-speakers in Woodham were his own pupils, and their efforts could not be much solace for him!

Then she recalled that Mr Harris had spoken to him in French. Well, there was nothing so very odd about that, for a much-travelled gentleman was likely to speak good French, surely? Why, at one time, everyone with any pretence to being in the higher ranks of Society spoke and wrote in French as a matter of course. It was only the war, the interminable war, which had put an end to that!

Then another puzzle occurred to her, brought to mind by the thought of the war. How did Mr Harris know so much about Colonel Congreve's rockets? The Colonel had once spoken about them at a dinner-party which she had attended, but not in the kind of detail about size and weight which Mr Harris had mentioned. The men who worked at the mill never mentioned them, and she doubted if most people in the town even knew of their existence.

The more she thought, the more puzzled and confused she became, and even praying did little to restore her peace of mind, for how could she be content when her whole heart longed for a man so enigmatic? Every aspect of him seemed filled with unanswerable questions which she could not resolve by asking him directly, for courtesy demanded that she phrase them in general terms, and he would certainly evade them, as he had always done so far. By no means could she ask the most important question of all, for how could a lady ask a man if he loved her?

Almost absent-mindedly, she went into the sanctuary to look at the altar-cloth, and found that it was now too dark to make out more than the vague whiteness of it. She ran her hands over its surface, feeling for drips of congealed candle-grease, for the Rector was sufficiently 'High' to have candles on the altar. She could detect none, but decided that she had better change the cloth in any case, and went to fetch a clean one from the vestry.

By the time she left the church, with the soiled cloth folded over her arm, and locked the door behind her, the sunset had faded to a band of greenish afterglow across the western horizon, and the area outside the church and down West Street was deserted, save for a solitary figure leaning on the rail of the footbridge, looking down into the stream.

It was Monsieur Roland, recognisable by his demi-bateau hat and the general set of him. He did not look up, or show any signs of awareness that there was another soul about in the town, so Lucinda assumed that he was deep in thought and did not disturb him.

She paused for a moment to look about her—at the swifts, still wheeling and crying round the church, the silent bats skimming the stream at the ford, and the pale candle-light in the windows above the shops in West Street—and then she went through the gate into the Rectory garden, where Fred was leaping about in pursuit of the moths amid the night-scented stocks in the border. He left this interesting occupation to come and roll about on the path before her feet, and she knelt beside him to rub his stomach, which he enjoyed.

'Oh, Fred!' she whispered. 'You like him too, don't you? If only . . . Why must I love such a difficult man? If only I could have fallen in love with Monsieur Roland, how much simpler everything would be! What am I to do?' But Fred only purred and butted his head against her, which was no help at all.

CHAPTER EIGHT

THE RECTOR had contrived, in the course of his visit to the metropolis, to obtain a new pair of spectacles which considerably improved his vision, but even with them on his nose, he failed to notice at breakfast the next morning that his daughter did not appear to have slept well, because he was too deeply immersed in a letter which had come for him from London. He tut-tutted and dear-deared over it from time to time, but said nothing to anyone of its contents; which was unusual, as he was given to confiding in Lucinda to a degree which, under other circumstances, he might have confided in his wife.

Lucinda was well aware that there was only one way to gather ripe mulberries if one did not wish to acquire in the process a pair of hands reminiscent of Lady Macbeth, so after breakfast she begged an old copy of the *Morning Post* from her father. This took a little time, as he had to consider which of his collection might be spared, and then glanced through the selected edition to make sure that it did not contain the report on the Battle of Trafalgar, or any other item of particular interest, but eventually he parted with most of one copy dating from 1791, which he thought he could manage without.

Disembowelling it as she went, Lucinda repaired to the garden and spread the separated sheets on the grass under a fruit-laden branch, then fetched the clothes-prop. By then, of course, Fred had searched under the paper to see if any rodents or beetles had taken refuge there, and she had to rearrange them before catching the end of the branch in the cleft of the prop and shaking it vigorously. A goodly rain of berries plopped down on the paper, and could then be tipped into a basin without Lucinda's fingers coming into contact with them at all. Fred consumed a few spare ones which had missed the papers, then strolled off to dig himself a few radishes in the vegetable plot.

Lucinda tied a cloth over the basin, called in on her mother, who was not yet downstairs, put on her shady chip-hat, debated over a shawl and decided to take it, despite the continuing warm weather, as there were several clouds about, and set out to call on Mrs Long.

The Colonel had rented a small house at the far end of West Street, near the imposing gates of the powder-mill, which were guarded by some of the soldiers from the camp. It was a neat little house, reminding Lucinda of the select dolls' residence which Amy had owned as a child, with a white front door under a fanlight, a brass knocker, two windows on either side of the door, five above (only the middle one was bricked up to avoid the window-tax) and three dormers on the roof. It even had a small walled garden at the back, and a branch of the stream which powered the powder-mill ran alongside it.

The maid who answered the door looked disconcerted at the sight of Lucinda, and said in nervous tones that she was not sure if Mrs Long was downstairs yet, but she would go and ask if she was At Home.

'Yes, very well. Tell her, please, that it's only to ask how she does,' Lucinda replied, wondering why the girl seemed so ill at ease. 'I'll wait in here.'

The maid darted forward ineffectually, but Lucinda had already passed her and opened the door of the parlour and stepped in before she could stop her, and the girl then hovered anxiously in the doorway, saying, 'Oh dear! Oh my! Oh dear!'

'That's all right,' said the room's occupant to her, in what was meant to be a reassuring tone, but his abrupt manner of speech frightened her even more, and she ran off, leaving the door open.

The gentleman stepped across from the window, where he had been standing, to close the door, then surveyed Lucinda's charming appearance appreciatively, and said, 'Good morning, Miss Calvert. How pleasant to meet you again!'

'Why, Sir Arthur!' Lucinda exclaimed. 'I thought you were in Ireland!' She smiled up at him, for he was half a foot taller than she, and seemed taller still, for his slim, scarlet-clad figure was stiffly upright. He had a very beaky nose, high arched brows, and a direct, no-nonsense manner. His normally haughty expression had softened at the sight of her, for the iron exterior which he habitually showed to friend and enemy alike covered a soft spot for a pretty female.

'We Wellesleys seldom stay in any one place for long,' he replied. 'Officially, I *am* in Ireland, but I've a little diversion afoot for the next few weeks. You'll not tell anyone I'm playing truant, I trust?'

Lucinda met his searching gaze and understood very well what he meant, but she replied in the same vein, 'I'll not breathe a word to a soul! I'd not wish to get you into trouble. I hoped, when I saw you here, and in uniform, that you might have returned to your old post at Hastings, for I'm sure we're far safer from any fear of a French invasion with you commanding the defences.'

'Ha h'm!' Sir Arthur Wellesley said modestly. 'Not much fear of that, since Trafalgar. Boney can't cross the Channel without a fleet to protect him, and he's short of ships. I don't think you need anticipate a plague of frogs in Woodham, unless he finds more men o' war from somewhere.'

'I wondered,' Lucinda confided. 'For there are so many more men in the camp, and the powder-mill is so busy.'

'Much talk, is there?' the General enquired.

'No, very little. The harvest is keeping the labouring people too busy to gossip, and the mill-men don't talk about their work. It's only the idle gentry who speak of it, and then after the price of hay, and the prospects for the shooting-season, and the latest fashions.'

There was a timid scratching at the door, and the poor maid called through it, 'Miss! Oh, miss! The Missis say, will you come up, if you please?'

'Coming, thank you!' Lucinda called back, then gave Sir Arthur her hand and said smilingly, 'I'm so glad *not* to have seen you again, and I wish you every success in your diversion. I shall pray for you.'

'Thankee, ma'am.' Sir Arthur kissed her hand gallantly, and held open the door for her, giving her a last conspiratorial wink as she went out, then closed it again behind her.

Mrs Long was, as the maid said, up but not down, which cryptic statement led Lucinda to go upstairs to the lady's bedroom, where she found her looking pallid and very tired, sitting in a comfortable chair by the open window.

'How kind of you to come,' she said. 'Will you excuse me from rising? I feel so dizzy when I stand up.'

'Should you not call the doctor?' Lucinda asked, for she thought Mrs Long looked really ill.

'It's always like this,' she replied with a wan smile. 'Only for a few weeks, thank goodness. I've had five, my dear, so I know how it will progress!'

'I brought the mulberries.' Lucinda put the cloth-covered basin on the dressing-table. 'Will you be able to eat them? The flavour is quite strong.'

'The nausea will pass off soon.' Mrs Long visibly brightened at the sight of the basin of fruit. 'I shall have them for my luncheon. I have such a liking for them, and it becomes a positive craving at this time! When I was 'carrying dear Henry—he's my third, you know—it was in winter, and I had to be content with raspberry jam, which is not entirely dissimilar, but neither is it the same, unfortunately! However, I made do, but I was eating it with a spoon, a whole gallipot at a time. The Colonel thought me run mad!'

She prattled on, mostly about her four sons and one daughter, who were all still in the schoolroom, for quite three-quarters of an hour, growing visibly better every moment, and by the time Lucinda left her she was quite herself again and thanked her caller very prettily for her time, and for the mulberries, and gave her a piece of lace which she had acquired in Malta, when the Colonel was stationed there.

As Lucinda went downstairs, she encountered the Colonel, who was hovering in the hall.

'I—er—um. . .' he began, looking embarrassed.

'Mrs Long seems quite well now,' Lucinda said smilingly, knowing very well that he was not waiting to speak to her about his wife's health. 'I believe my mother knows a good tisane for the morning sickness, which may help, so I'll let her have the receipt.'

'Yes. Thank you.' The Colonel brushed these trivialities aside. 'About your—er—encounter . . .' He seemed at a loss how to go on, so Lucinda took pity on him and said, 'Encounter, Colonel? I encountered no one. I called to see Mrs Long, and have been with her this past hour.'

'Quite so!' said the Colonel, looking relieved. 'Just the thing! Thank you, Miss Calvert; most kind of you. I'm sure my poor dear wife appreciated your visit.' And he beamed upon Lucinda as he showed her to the door himself, and stood watching her walk away up the street.

A few paces from the Longs' front door, she saw Mr Jones coming towards her, and it was immediately apparent that he was walking on air, for his steps had a joyful elasticity, and his normally serious, thoughtful face was split by a broad grin.

'Miss Lucinda!' he exclaimed, fairly rushing to meet her and seizing both her hands. 'I'm the happiest man in the world, and all thanks to you! Had you not spoken, I might still be sunk in despair, or even enlisted in the navy!'

'Congratulations!' Lucinda cried, her face alight with pleasure. 'Did you really go *at once* to Mr Martin? What did he say?'

'He seemed a little surprised at first, but I simply blurted out, "I shall have two thousand a year when I marry, on top of the one thousand I already enjoy, as well as my stipend, and I wish to marry your daughter." He said, "Well done!" and shook my hand, then called dearest Amaryllis!'

'And what did Amy say?' Lucinda prompted, for he seemed to have fallen into a delightful stupor in contemplation of the magical syllables.

'Mr Martin said to her, "Here is Mr Jones come to ask you to marry him. What do you say to that, then?" and she said, "Yes!" Who would have believed it could all be so simple!' and he danced a little jig of excitement.

'Mr Jones! Miss Enston is staring at you most disapprovingly,' Lucinda whispered sharply. 'Pray behave yourself! You'd best go and tell her the news, before she tells everyone you've run mad or gone over to Rome!'

'As if I'd do that!' Mr Jones exclaimed ebulliently. 'Why, they'd not let me marry darling, darling Amaryllis! Is it not a beautiful name, Miss Lucinda? A-mar-yll-is! Sheer poetry! Yes, yes!'—raising his hands to fend off further reproaches—'I go—I go at once! Miss Enston, a word, if you please!' Then he was off across the street towards the surprised and disapproving figure on the other side.

Lucinda walked on, feeling a bitter-sweet pleasure in the Curate's joy, and looked back to see him talking earnestly to Miss Enston, whose face was now wreathed in smiles. The next moment, Lucinda collided with Monsieur Roland, who had just stepped out of the post office with an open newspaper held before his face.

There were, of course, profuse apologies on both sides, and then he said, 'You were abroad early this morning, Miss Calvert. I trust there is nothing amiss?'

'No, nothing at all,' she replied, wishing her words were true, but knowing that he could not be referring to her private problems.

'I thought per'aps—you are coming from the direction of the powder-mill . . .'

'Oh, you'd have heard if there was any trouble there,' Lucinda assured him. 'It usually makes a very loud bang!'

'But there was so much activity there yesterday, and again this morning.' He was apparently unamused by her small joke. 'I was passing yesterday, after I met you, and found the river covered with—what do you call them? Large, shallow boats . . .'

'Barges,' Lucinda supplied. 'I expect they were moving a stock of powder, or perhaps bringing in materials. I've just been to call on Mrs Long, for she's not feeling quite the thing at present.'

'Poor lady! She must 'ave many anxieties!'

'Anxieties?' She wondered what he meant.

'With 'er 'usband a soldier. War is very 'ard on soldiers' wives and mothers, Miss Calvert.'

'True, but our army isn't actually fighting anyone at present, is it?' Lucinda pointed out. 'We can't fight your horrid Bonaparte when we can't get at him, can we?' She hoped that she was not sounding too ingenuous, for the last remark, in her own ears, seemed quite imbecile, but the Frenchman smiled tolerantly and replied, ''E is not my 'orrid Bonaparte! I disown 'im! I 'ope you enjoyed your riding yesterday? It is long since I saw you on 'orseback.'

'Yes, I've not been able to ride since poor old Pickle died. It was very kind of Mr Harris to lend his horses. We had a most enjoyable afternoon.'

'It must be pleasant to be rich, and able to give pleasure to beautiful young ladies,' he said with melancholy gallantry. 'Ah, if only t'ings could be as they once were for me, I too could offer you 'orses, and all the riches of Ind!' His dark eyes turned on her in a sentimental manner which she found quite disturbing.

'Oh heavens,' she thought. 'It's bad enough that a glance from Mr Harris turns me to a jelly, but I cannot cope with feeling peculiar if Monsieur Roland looks at me as well! And why do I find myself speaking to him like a ninny-hammer?'

'Have you heard the good news about Mr Jones?' she asked hastily. 'He is engaged to be married.'

'So even the poor Curate 'as found 'is lady!' Monsieur Roland looked more melancholy and lonely than ever. 'I wish 'im joy, for it must be a great 'appiness to win the lady of your choice!' He sighed deeply. 'Miss Martin, I suppose?' he added on a more down-to-earth note.

'Yes. I must go and see her before luncheon.' Lucinda

glanced up at the church clock, which already showed past eleven.

'I'll walk with you as far as the church, if I may.' He fell into step beside her and they walked up West Street towards the stream.

'A curious arrangement,' he commented, gesturing towards the ford with his folded newspaper. 'I wonder that no one 'as thought to build a proper bridge, for it's 'ardly convenient to 'ave the town cut in two like this.'

'I expect someone will, one day,' Lucinda replied. 'As long as the footbridge is kept in good repair, we manage well enough, and the ford is hardly ever too deep for an easy crossing. Did you say you were going to the church?'

'Yes. It's peaceful there, and your father is kind enough to allow me to go in, despite our differences of faith.'

'Yes, it's a very pleasant building.' Lucinda answered absently in words which she would never normally have applied to the church, but her attention had been distracted by the sound of tramping feet behind them. She turned to watch as a long column of soldiers marched past, brave in their red coats, muskets at the slope and buttons gleaming. She wondered how they would reduce their four-abreast formation to cross the narrow footbridge, but they simply marched through the ford as if there was no water there.

'I see what you mean about the bridge,' she said to Monsieur Roland, but he was watching the soldiers and did not hear her.

'So many men!' he said. 'Where can they be going?'

'I expect they're just marching for practice,' she replied, but the column was followed by a line of baggage wagons, so she knew that this was something more than a route-march.

'Did Colonel Long not say that some of 'is men were leaving? I 'ope they 'ave found some way of getting at Bonaparte! Oh, if only that man could be defeated! If only *ma pauvre belle France* could be set free! Ah, Miss Calvert, I shall go, as your good father so kindly allows, into your fine church to pray for my country.'

'Yes, by all means,' she said, sounding so inane in her own estimation that she marvelled that the Frenchman could have such a devastating effect on her conversational powers. They picked their way over the footbridge, and she left him at the church door, then hastened up the churchyard path, anxious to hear Amy's report on Mr Jones and his proposal.

The market square was like a beehive about to swarm, for the market was in full swing, and men were working on the ruins of the two burned shops, clearing away the wreckage ready to start rebuilding. Lucinda paused to buy some spools of thread and a paper of pins from the haberdasher, some plump blush-cheeked apricots and a melon from the fruiterer, and to exchange greetings with various acquaintances, working her way steadily through the crowd towards the Martins' house, where the footman informed her that Miss Martin was above-stairs in her room, and expecting her.

Lucinda, surprised to hear that Amy was not yet down, hastened to her bedroom, thinking she might be ill, but found her friend kneeling on the floor amid a scattering of gowns, frocks, gloves, slippers and stockings, reviewing her wardrobe.

She got up quickly as Lucinda entered, and ran to embrace her, laughing and flushed about the cheeks. 'Have you heard?' she said. 'It's quite incredible, and I've you to thank for it!'

'Mr Jones told me, just now.' Lucinda was all smiles at her friend's happiness. 'He was bouncing along West

Street, four feet above the pavement, and grinning like a crocodile! I'm so happy for you, Amy!'

The two young ladies sat down on the bed, and Amy gave Lucinda a detailed account of the previous evening's events, from the knock at the front door, the footman's entry into the parlour to request Mr Martin to spare a few minutes to talk to Mr Jones, then the puzzled wait, wondering what Mr Jones might have come about, hoping and despairing by turns.

'I nearly died, Lucy!' she exclaimed. 'I had a feeling that it was not just parish business, but at the same time I didn't really believe that he could have come about *that*, and yet all the afternoon he'd been looking at me in such a way, and looking away again, and sighing! Mama would keep talking about the dinner-party she's planning, and there was I, straining my ears to hear the slightest sound from Papa's study . . . And then at last—oh, hours afterwards, it must have been quite ten minutes!—at last, in they came, and Papa said Mr Jones wished to marry me, and what did I think? So I said "Yes", and Mama had the vapours, just a little, at the shock, but more because I hadn't made any maidenly hesitations! She kept saying that she couldn't think how a daughter of hers could be so bold and brazen, and Mr Jones just held my hand and *looked* at me, and said never a word. Well, he didn't need to, of course, for it was all in his eyes! Then at last he got back his senses, and told me it was all your doing, for he was quite in despair, and had just decided to resign and join the navy when you said just the right thing to him, so he came at once to ask. Oh, Lucy! I'm so happy! And even Mama is pleased, for it turns out that he's not a poor clergyman at all, but we shall be quite comfortably settled! Isn't it amazing?' And there was more hugging and kissing and laughing with the excitement of it all.

Lucinda was late for luncheon again, but her mother was mollified by the good news she brought and forgot to complain about the lateness, although, once the first exclamations and expressions of pleasure had been uttered and the obvious questions asked, she spoke plaintively about the difficulties of marrying off a daughter who made all her efforts on behalf of others and not of herself.

'I'd no idea that Mr Jones had such good prospects,' she said. 'I'd have given him much more encouragement if I'd realised! Really, Lucinda, fancy letting him escape you—nay—worse than that! Actually encouraging him into the arms of Amaryllis Martin! You really must try harder, you know, or you'll be left unwed. Why do you not resolve to attach Captain Bridges, or even Mr Harris, before the summer is over?'

Lucinda was saved from further mortification by the Rector, who looked severely at his wife through his new spectacles and said, 'Mrs Calvert, my dear! The match between Miss Martin and Mr Jones is clearly one of deep mutual feeling, and I should wish Lucinda to make one of the same sort. I'll not have her sold off to the highest bidder, like a prize pig! Let her wait until she finds a man for whom she can feel deeply, and, so he's worthy of her, I've no doubt the Lord will provide for them both. And'—changing the subject abruptly—'talking of the Lord providing, a fine amount of money has been subscribed for the fire victims, but both of the shopkeepers were well insured, and they have both said that they would wish their shares to be divided between the poor Howes and the purchase of the new engine, with the result that we have enough for a second engine of a smaller size! Is that not good news?'

'They say that bad news goes in threes,' observed Mrs Calvert, somewhat subdued by the early part of her husband's speech, 'so let us hope that it also applies to good news.'

The third piece of news reached Lucinda on Sunday morning, after she had spent the service trying to keep her mind on its proper pursuit instead of gazing soulfully at Mr Harris, who sat brightly alert in his pew with his eyes fixed firmly either on his Prayer Book or on Mr Jones, whose turn it was to take Mattins. After the service, however, he was slow to leave his place, and joined Lucinda as she walked down the nave after her customary few words with Mr Gibbs.

'Good morning, Miss Calvert,' he said, looking at her with a distinct twinkle in his eyes, so that she feared he had guessed how much turmoil four simple everyday words were causing in her breast. 'You'll be pleased to hear that the villainous Mr Marshall proved quite mild and agreeable, and viewed my proposition favourably. The Cob-Enders may work for me, yet continue to live in his wretched hovels until next quarter-day, when they must leave. As the new cottages will be finished by the end of this month, they will have the whole of September to move.'

'That is wonderful!' Lucinda exclaimed. 'Mama was right—she said that there would be three pieces of good news!'

'What are the other two?'

Lucinda had impulsively held out her hand to him as she spoke, and he had taken hold of it, but did not let it go again, so she answered him in a confused fashion which might have led a less intelligent man to apprehend that Mr Jones could afford to buy a second fire-engine, and the Rector was to marry Miss Martin.

'Ah,' said Mr Harris, smiling in his ironical fashion and easing his grip on her hand just enough for her to withdraw it, 'so that's why you wished him to accompany us on Friday. I suspected that you might have designs on him yourself!'

'Oh, no!' Lucinda exclaimed. 'I don't . . . He's not . . . Not at all! Oh dear!'

Mr Harris looked as if he might be about to burst into unseemly laughter, but he restrained himself until they had reached the porch, where Arthur rose from a position of recumbent despair by the outer door and came to greet his master as if he had been ten years gone into the church. Mr Harris patted him and informed him that Mr Jones was to marry Miss Martin, and was not, therefore, to be bitten.

'I'm sure so fine a dog had no such evil intention!' protested Mr Jones, who was standing by the door. He eyed Arthur a trifle nervously when the dog padded over to him, but was quite charmed when he licked his hand. 'There's a good boy, and named after a great king! A great *Welsh* king!' he added impressively.

'Oh, but he's . . .' Lucinda checked herself, not wishing even to name Sir Arthur Wellesley after the General's request that she should not mention him. Mr Harris caught her eye and winked, and she realised that he thought she had broken off to spare Mr Jones's Celtic feelings.

'The trouble with having a spotted dog,' he said reflectively, 'is that the sight of him reminds me of the other sort—the edible variety—and around luncheon time that makes me hungry, so I'll bid you good day. I wish you joy, Mr Jones, and hearty congratulations! Miss Calvert!' He put on his beaver hat at a jaunty angle and set off towards the Black Swan to fetch his carriage, Arthur walking conscientiously at his heels.

Lucinda watched him go, then realised that Mr Jones was looking at her in a thoughtful fashion, at which she flushed, bade him a hasty farewell, and fairly ran home to the Rectory.

Despite the fact that he had obviously waited to speak to her after the service, Lucinda felt disappointed by Mr Harris's abrupt departure, and had a vague, uneasy feeling all the afternoon that he might call, but he did not, and the one time the doorbell rang, it was only Mr Gibbs, come to beg the loan of Fred's tail to lay on a sty on his eyelid. Fred made no objection, but Mr Calvert pointed out that it was all superstition, and in any case, Fred was not entirely black, but booted and cravated with white.

It was natural that Lucinda should wish to visit the Cob-Enders to find out how they felt about their latest piece of good fortune, but she did not expect to have the opportunity to do so for several days. However, instead of going to call on Mrs Long again on Monday afternoon, as she intended, she found that the lady was so much recovered that she proposed herself for the afternoon to spend some time in a comfortable chat with Mrs Calvert, so Lucinda had some unexpected free time.

Not wishing to go to Cob End empty-handed, she filled her basket with some more baby-clothes which had been left at the Rectory for charitable purposes, begged a couple of loaves, some jam and the last of Sunday's mutton from Cook, and set off on her usual route, meeting more folk than she expected, for harvest was now going on apace in the lower fields.

Naturally she hoped that she might encounter Mr Harris somewhere in his fields, or perhaps along the Selvedge, but all she met on his land were his newly arrived cows, a fine-looking herd of about twenty, some of them in calf, who gazed at her with the usual curiosity of their kind, but hardly pausing from tearing at the lush grass.

She meant to stay only a short while at Cob End, but she found that the joyful atmosphere there was a little muted by the fact that Mrs Graygoose's three-month-old baby was ill with thrush, and no one seemed to know what to do about it, so Lucinda must set to work to make a strong infusion of thyme, which fortunately grew in wild profusion on a near-by bank, and clean out the poor child's mouth with it, instructing the mother to continue the treatment until the white matter ceased to form.

Hardly had she finished that than one of the Warrener boys was brought home by his friends with a broken arm, having fallen from a tree.

Lucinda's first reaction was to send someone for Dr Roberts, but there was a horrified outcry at the idea, for all the Cob-Enders were convinced that a doctor would cut off the arm as a matter of course, for they all knew that doctors did no good at all, and their patients always ended up worse off, if not dead, and, besides, they cost a great deal of money. As all attempts to argue the point failed, she took another look at the arm and discovered that only one of the two forearm bones was broken, and not much displaced, so, after a little thought and some very intensive prayer, she carefully straightened the arm, gently pushing and pulling at the broken bone, which, fortunately, had not punctured the skin. Meanwhile, Mr Warrener, summoned from his rabbits by his anxious wife, smoothed two pieces of wood for splints, and Mrs Warrener bound strips of a very old shirt round them for padding.

Two of the little girls had been sent out to seek comfrey leaves, and a thick wet paste of them was made and laid on a piece of the shirt-tail and wrapped round the bruised area, and then the splints were put above and below the forearm and firmly bandaged into place.

'That's the best I can do,' Lucinda said doubtfully.

'You was capital, miss, and never 'urt at all!' insisted the patient, who had fainted twice and now had a peculiarly greenish-white face, but was full of game spirit and already looked forward to boasting about his adventure.

'I don't know how we shall ever thank you enough, ma'am,' said Mrs Warrener, weeping a little. 'I'll make us all a good strong cup of tea!' Which she did, and Lucinda was glad of it, although it tasted odd, for it was really made with a little tea mixed with a lot of herbs.

What with one thing and another, by the time she was ready to leave for home, it was already dark. Of course Mr Warrener offered to walk home with her, but he looked tired, and had not yet had his evening meal, so Lucinda declined, saying that she would do very well by herself, for the moon was up and near full. Mrs Warrener lent her a little horn lantern with a tallow candle in it, which gave a dim light, and she set off without the slightest anticipation of any difficulty.

She was not a nervous female, and the countryside held no fears for her. In fact, she enjoyed walking across the fields at night, and even the eerie cry of a barn owl, or the sight of its pale shape drifting across the night, did not startle or alarm her. There was enough light to see her path fairly clearly, except when it ran among the trees, and she had no trouble crossing the bridge over the stream.

It was not until she reached the point on the Selvedge where Mr Harris had set up the oak log for a seat, just before the woodland path came down to join the Selvedge, that she heard anything unusual. It was the clink of a horse's hoof against a stone, and before she had identified it, she heard voices as well.

She stopped in her tracks, for she knew at once who was most likely to be abroad at night, well away from the turnpikes, and with horses, and it was best not to encounter any of the smuggling fraternity in case they were not the local men, who knew she would do them no harm. She expected that they would either go ahead of her, down to the town, or the other way, up into the Forest, so she stepped aside from the path and knelt down behind a thickly-leaved bush, hiding the dim glow of the lantern under her upturned basket. A low branch pushed her bonnet off, but she let it go, for the strings still held it at her neck, and it hung down her back.

The voices, which were subdued, drew nearer, and she made out the dark shapes of four ponies and half a dozen men. They did not turn up into the Forest, but stopped at the junction of the paths and stood about as if waiting for someone.

'Why ain't 'e 'ere?' one man muttered.

'Don't be so bloody impatient! 'Tain't time yet!' said a more authoritative voice, apparently of the leader of the group. 'Church clock ain't struck the hour yet. 'Ere 'e comes now! Is the watch set?'

'Yes, course it is!' said another voice. ''Arry's on watch.'

Lucinda did not hear anyone come along the path to join the smugglers, but she saw them turn as if to greet a newcomer, and then another dark figure appeared and said, 'Good evening, gentlemen, I trust I've not kept you waiting?'

The voice was pleasant, cultivated, and quite unmistakable. The newcomer was Mr Harris! Lucinda gasped and leaned forward, desperate to learn what dealings someone so new to the district might have with the smugglers, and how he came to be on such apparently good terms with them. She was quite unaware that 'Arry, who was on watch, had come along within the shelter of the trees and was standing just behind her, and the sudden blow on her head was totally unexpected. The worst of it was deflected by her piled-up hair, but it was still hard enough to send her sprawling down on the path, and for a few moments everything went black.

As her senses returned, she was vaguely aware of anxious voices, and particularly of Mr Harris saying sharply, 'What did you do a dam' fool thing like that for? You might have killed her!' She stirred slightly, and a hand clamped over her mouth for a moment, so briefly that, in her confusion, she was hardly certain that it had actually done so, but some instinct for self-preservation made her lie still and keep her eyes closed.

'Well, she were spying on us!' said a defensive voice.

'More likely hiding from you, if she heard you coming!' Mr Harris replied scornfully. 'You don't imagine the Preventive Officers are recruiting females, do you?'

'Couldn't see she were female.' The defensive voice now sounded sulky. ''Twere dark under them trees.'

'What's she doing 'ere, out in the fields after dark?' asked another voice.

'Returning home after a charitable visit to Cob End, of course. Don't you recognise her?' asked Mr Harris with some asperity. 'Here, shine the glim on her a moment.' A gleam of light flashed momentarily across Lucinda's closed eyelids. 'There, see? It's the Rector's daughter!'

'Omigawd!' exclaimed a voice which sounded familiar to Lucinda, but which she could not quite place from what was effectively only one word.

''Ow was 'Arry to know?' asked the leader, sounding both alarmed and truculent. 'You know the risk we run! 'Ow could we expect it to be 'er? You know 'ow we 'as to deal with folk as might peach on us.'

'And how many times do I have to tell you that your

necks are perfectly safe as long as you do as I tell you?'
Mr Harris replied crisply. 'Take the letter—here it
is—and give me the other one. Now, be off with you!'

'What about 'er?' asked 'Arry. 'What'll you do with
'er?'

'You can safely leave me to dispose of the evidence.
Get on your way, and a safe journey to you!'

With apparent reluctance the smugglers began to
move, but then 'Arry, who did not seem very quick on
the uptake, suddenly said shrilly, 'What do 'e mean—
dispose of the evidence? 'Ere, 'e's not going ter do
anything 'armful, is 'e?'

'Don't be so blamed stupid!' said the leader irately.
''E's a gentleman, ain't 'e? And keep yer voice down, or
they'll 'ear you in 'Orsing!'

'Will she be all right?' 'Arry persisted in a hoarse
whisper.

'Yes,' Mr Harris replied tersely. 'Now get on, or you'll
miss the tide.'

This appeared to satisfy even 'Arry, for the sounds of
men and horses receded into the Forest and died away,
and Lucinda ventured to open her eyes.

CHAPTER NINE

LUCINDA HAD been aware for some time that she was lying on the path, half-supported against a human body, and the arms attached to that body were holding her quite gently, while a hand had made a brief examination by touch of her head, which was tender at one point. She now discovered that the body, arms and hand belonged to Mr Harris, for everyone else had gone.

She thought it safe to utter a small moan and show signs of recovering consciousness, but the results surprised her, for Mr Harris exclaimed, 'Oh, thank God!' in a highly theatrical manner, clasped her to him, and planted a kiss on her brow.

'Where am I?' she enquired in a faint voice, and followed that with the other question always asked by heroines in novels on recovering from a dead faint, 'What happened?'

'Don't you remember?' Mr Harris asked, apparently recovered from his fit of theatrics, for he spoke in a normal fashion and moved away a little, only supporting her lightly with an arm about her shoulders.

'I—I remember walking along the path . . .' she replied slowly. 'There was an owl flying across the field . . . I was watching it . . .' She stopped and waited to hear his response.

'Then I suppose you tripped and fell,' he said, sounding only the merest trifle tentative, 'and struck your head.'

'How did you come to be near?' She kept her voice vague and low.

'I often take a walk about the fields in the evening,' he replied. 'I found you lying on the path. Can you stand up, do you think?'

She did so without any ill effect, and then he helped her to the log seat, where she looked about her and asked, 'What became of my basket and Mrs Warrener's lantern?'

'They're here.' He brought them from the side of the path, where Lucinda had certainly not left them. Her bonnet had been removed, so he brought her that as well, and she put it on.

'I don't think you're much hurt, for I couldn't find any damage but a bump—no blood,' he said. 'Er . . .' more tentatively, 'were you actually—um—unconscious, do you think?'

'Yes,' Lucinda replied firmly. 'I think I must have been, for a few moments, at least.' It was, she assured herself, quite true. She then had a fleeting recollection of a hand placed over her mouth, and wondered if he thought she had been pretending all the time. 'Yes, I'm certain I was, for I don't remember you coming upon me.'

He apparently accepted her statement, for he showed considerably more concern than heretofore, and examined her head again with much more care, then said a little doubtfully, 'I still don't think you've suffered any real damage, but I'd like to take a look in a better light. I think you'd best come to the house, so that I can make sure, and then I'll take you home. Leave your basket and lantern; I'll send someone to collect them in the morning.'

Lucinda agreed, for she felt more than a little shaky, partly from the blow on the head, but mostly from the shock of what she had overhead. She stood up, and thought she could walk as far as Pinnacles if she took his arm, but he picked her up and carried her, silencing her not very vehement protests with a brisk, 'Nonsense, my dear girl! You're no great weight, and I'll take a rest when I need one.'

It should have been a great pleasure to Lucinda to be in his arms, but her head was aching, and her thoughts were disturbing. She could not even understand her own motives in not telling him what she could remember. Obviously it had been sensible to feign unconsciousness while the smugglers were still there, but surely Mr Harris would do her no harm if she told him the truth? His remark about disposing of the evidence was a joke, was it not? There must be some simple explanation for his meeting with the smugglers—after all, perfectly respectable people had dealings with contrabanders, although they were a very cautious and suspicious group for the good reason that their lives were at risk. It was surprising, though, that they should already be on familiar terms with someone who had been in the district less than a month, and apparently taking instructions from him, for he had told them to go, not asked them.

After a while her thoughts turned to the most curious part of the whole business—the mention of letters. What letters could they possibly be? It wasn't unusual to ask a friend to take a letter to someone, if he or she happened to be going near to where the recipient lived, but somehow Lucinda could not imagine that smugglers were now defrauding the Post Office as well as the Customs and Excise. Mr Harris had mentioned two letters, as far as she could make out—one he was sending, and one he was receiving. It seemed very odd that a wealthy man should not use the normal postal service, for it only cost a shilling or so to receive a letter.

Her thoughts grew more and more confused, and it was a relief when they were interrupted by Mr Harris saying, 'I think I'll take a brief rest here, if you don't mind,' and putting her down carefully on the top of the flight of steps from the Selvedge path to the lowest terrace of his garden. 'You're very quiet,' he added. 'How do you feel?'

'My head is a little sore, but that's all.'

'What were you doing along the Selvedge at this time of night? It's long past dinner-time, I believe, and I doubt you've been dining at Cob End.'

'I went there for a brief visit, between tea and dinner,' she said ruefully, 'but encountered a chapter of accidents,' and then told him about the baby with thrush and Billy Warrener's broken arm.

'And you set it yourself? Why did you not send for a surgeon?'

'There's only Dr Roberts in Woodham, and he's a physician,' she explained. 'And they don't trust doctors. I suppose it's because they never call a doctor until it's really too late for him to do anything. Besides, they can't afford to pay him.'

'There's a competent surgeon at the army camp,' Mr Harris said thoughtfully. 'You might have known I'd pay the fee.'

'I didn't think . . .' Lucinda began, and then, before she could stop herself, 'How did you know there's a surgeon at the camp? I didn't!'

'In fact, I doubt if he'd charge, as it's a child. He is quite well paid by the War Office.'

'How do you know?' Lucinda persisted, feeling that she could not cope with another unexplained mystery that evening.

'I believe the army gives a reasonable rate of remuneration to a skilled man with specialised knowledge.' Mr Harris sounded a trifle puzzled by the question. 'Since the Duke of York's reforms, you know, they've attempted to coax good surgeons into the service. One of his concerns was the lack of qualified surgeons in the army, and the only way to get them was to pay them at least what they might expect to receive in private practice. Shall we go on? I don't wish you to take a chill by sitting about in the night air.'

Lucinda gave up trying to get an answer out of him, for she was beginning to feel a little overwrought, what with one thing and another, but she said, almost tearfully, as he picked her up again, 'If you know him, I wish you might ask him to look at Billy's arm, if you can persuade his parents to allow it, for I'm afraid something will go wrong unless he has proper attention.'

'It shall be done,' he said soothingly. 'I promise you I'll send to him first thing in the morning, and the Warreners will, I think, do as I ask them, so don't give it another thought.'

It took Lucinda a few minutes to get her emotions under proper control again and stop herself from actually dissolving into tears, and by then Mr Harris had carried her up the terraces and in at the open french doors on the garden side of the house, but into a small breakfast parlour, not the grand salon. It was a pleasant and comparatively small room, with a round table and a few chairs, lit by a single branch of candles which stood on the table.

'Now, let me put you down here,' he said, depositing her gently in a chair, 'and do you catch your breath for a moment.'

There was a movement in the shadows on the far side of the room, and a dark-clad man came forward into the light, saying anxiously, 'What's happened? Who's this?'

He was a complete stranger to Lucinda—a small, sharp-featured man with thin greying hair and uneven yellowish teeth—and she thought he did not look at all a pleasant person, or the sort of guest she would have expected Mr Harris to be entertaining. Even his speech sounded wrong, for he had a distinctly common accent.

'Nothing to concern you,' Mr Harris replied, not quite sounding curt, but very near it. 'The lady is a friend who has suffered a slight accident. It need not detain you, however, for I'm sure you're anxious to be on your way.'

'What about the . . .?' the man began, but Mr Harris cut in smoothly, 'The papers? Here they are.' He produced a small packet which, to Lucinda, looked very much like a letter, for it was folded and sealed exactly as a letter would have been.

The man took the packet and stowed it away carefully inside his coat. 'Then I'll be off, and leave you to your—er . . .'

'You'll forgive me if I don't see you off,' Mr Harris said politely, ringing the bell. 'Ah, George'—as the footman entered before the bell could have stopped ringing—'the gentleman is just leaving. Good night to you, sir!' He bowed just sufficiently to the man, who gave an equally slight bow back, and departed.

'Who was that?' Lucinda asked in a small voice, not really expecting an answer.

'A reformed rogue,' Mr Harris replied lightly. 'But not so much reformed that I don't instruct the servants to keep an eye on him! Now, let me see that bump.'

He moved the candles nearer to Lucinda, removed her bonnet, and gently parted her hair over the painful area. She winced slightly in anticipation, but his fingers moved carefully about the bump without actually touching it, pressing slightly.

'No sign of any damage, thank God. In fact, even the bump is but a slight one. I'm surprised that you were unconscious for so long.'

'I don't know how long it was,' Lucinda answered shrewdly, thinking to disconcert him, but he answered, 'If it was long enough for you not to have heard me coming, and, indeed, for me to discover you, utter various exclamations of alarm and despondency and— er . . .' He broke off, and Lucinda, who happened to be looking up at his face, was surprised to see a flicker of something like embarrassment pass across it. She then recollected what else he had done, and blushed.

There was a moment's silence as Mr Harris looked at her, and then he said, 'It's quite amazing how odd a person's reactions can be to a shock. I've always considered myself a level-headed fellow, but . . . well, there you are! I think I'd best take you home soon, but a dish of tea first. It will do us both good.'

He rang the bell again, adding as he did so, 'I'll not offer you brandy, for it's not advisable after a blow on the head.'

George was presumably still disposing of the mysterious visitor, for another servant answered the bell and was despatched for tea and to order Mr Harris's phaeton brought round. While they were waiting, Mr Harris, presumably recollecting a useful piece of information, requested Lucinda to hold out her right hand before her, at arm's length.

'Now,' he said when she had complied, looking at him rather puzzled, 'in one movement, lay your forefinger on the end of your nose.'

She did so, utterly mystified, and he said cheerfully, 'Well, if what I recall is correct, that means you are not concussed.'

The tea arrived very promptly, accompanied by a

prosperous-looking Charlotte who greeted her old friend in a perfunctory fashion, and looked expectantly at Mr Harris, who poured tea for Lucinda and himself, and set a dish of milk on the floor for the cat.

'She nearly always comes with the tea-tray,' he said, smiling down on the animal.

'Is she proving satisfactory?' Lucinda asked, gratefully sipping her tea, which was far superior to any that poor Mrs Warrener could ever have afforded, and was remarkably soothing to her jangled nerves.

'Eminently! There was immense slaughter for the first few days after her arrival, but now she has little to do but police the premises, which she does with great attention. You're an excellent female, are you not, Charlotte?'

The cat looked up at the sound of her name, which she seemed to have learned already, and made a brief remark which sounded like an affirmative before returning to an assiduous polishing of her dish, and that topic of conversation being exhausted, silence descended on the room. Lucinda would very much have liked to break it, for she felt it was rapidly becoming oppressive, but the only words she could think of were a string of questions, and her head was too sore and confused to be able to phrase them tactfully, so she drank her tea, and then set down her cup and dish on the table.

'I think,' said Mr Harris, 'that I'd best lend you a cloak, for the night air is chill, and that shawl is not over-thick. Shall we go?'

Lucinda stood up without turning giddy, and with some support from Mr Harris, which was not entirely necessary, went out into the hall, where a warm cloak was draped round her shoulders. It was too long, of course, for it appeared to be his own, but he carried the excess like a train as they went out to his phaeton. He settled her, with some help from his tiger, on the high perch seat alongside him, then took the ribbons, waited for the tiger to mount behind, then set the vehicle in motion, driving carefully and obviously watching the driveway for any unevenness which might cause a lurch, for the moonlight was now so bright that it was possible to make out the individual pieces of gravel.

'I think,' he said presently, 'that it would be advisable for you to move closer, and let me put an arm about you, for you might turn faint and fall off. It's quite a distance to the ground.'

Lucinda thought his argument specious at first, for she did not feel in the least faint, but then she recalled that he believed her to have been unconscious for some time, so she obediently moved up and was encircled comfortably by his arm, which did not appear to discommode his driving in the least.

They soon reached the lodge gates and turned out on to the road, which, being turnpiked, was well surfaced, and the phaeton picked up a little speed as the horses moved from a walk to a trot. The hedges sped by on either side, shadowy and mysterious in the moonlight, which turned the road to a ribbon of silver. The carriage-lamps shone on the glossy rumps of the horses, a fine pair of sorrels, and there was no sound but the steady clop of their hooves, the grind of the wheels, and the occasional night sounds—the cry of an owl, the strange churring of a nightjar, and the crack of its wings as it took flight at their approach.

It was only the second time that Lucinda had been driven in a phaeton, and she so much enjoyed the lightness and speed of the vehicle, the comforting arm round her waist, and the nearness of the man beside her, that she temporarily set aside her doubts and uncertainties until, all too soon, the sound of the wheels changed as they came upon the stones of the town streets and sped down past the churchyard, and drew up before the Rectory.

Mr Calvert came hastening out of the front door as Mr Harris helped Lucinda to descend, exclaiming, 'Why, what has happened? Why are you so late?'

'There's been a slight accident,' Mr Harris replied. 'Nothing serious, but I think perhaps Dr Roberts might be summoned.'

He took Lucinda's arm and led her into the house, and to the parlour, the Rector backing and filling behind like a sheepdog. Mrs Calvert, who was reclining in her usual languid fashion on a sofa, immediately became galvanised into action. Within minutes, it was Lucinda who was reclining on the sofa, Annie had been sent for the doctor, Mr Harris and the Rector had a glass of cognac apiece, and a promise of coffee to follow as soon as Cook could have it brewed, and the stage was set for explanations.

To Lucinda's relief, Mr Harris told the story, recounting the episodes of the thrush and the broken arm, which explained Lucinda's late departure from Cob End, Mr Warrener's offer to walk with her and her reasons for declining, the matter of the owl, and Mr Harris's discovery of her unconscious form. It was told so smoothly and convincingly that Lucinda almost believed it herself, and was thankful that she had been spared the necessity of admitting the truth in front of him, for she could never have brought herself to lie to her parents.

'Luckily I usually take a stroll after dinner,' he added. 'I thought it best to take her to the house until I could be sure that there was no serious injury, and then I drove her down. I think she has only a bump on her head, but it's as well to make sure.'

Mrs Calvert thanked him with a proper degree of gratitude but a minimum of fuss, inspected Lucinda's head, and fetched arnica and a rag with which to apply it, and then Dr Roberts arrived.

He was a stout man with an aldermanic look about the waistcoat but experienced in the field of minor accidents, and a brief examination, larded with Latin terms for effect, and including, to Lucinda's private amusement, the same test already tried by Mr Harris of touching the end of her nose (but carried out with more pomp) soon led him to state quite firmly that she had struck her head against a hard object and sustained the very mildest concussion, which a day spent quietly in her room would soon put right. He then accepted a glass of cognac and a cup of coffee, which was now ready, chatted pleasantly of this and that while he drank them, then produced a folded paper of powder from his bag and gave it to Mrs Calvert.

'This is a mild sleeping-draught,' he said. 'I would advise that Miss Calvert takes it now and retires. A good night's rest will do wonders.' With that, he departed.

Lucinda, who was feeling that the quiet of her own room would be very welcome, took her draught stirred into hot milk—it was unpleasantly bitter, but a couple of sugar-biscuits which her mother kindly had ready took away the taste—and thanked Mr Harris for his kindness.

'I'll send your basket down in the morning,' he assured her, holding the hand she had proffered, 'and return Mrs Warrener's lantern. I'll not forget about the surgeon for Billy. There's nothing need cause you any uneasiness, so I beg you'll not worry yourself about a thing. I promise you everything will be well.'

The sleeping-draught seemed to taking effect already, for Lucinda hardly took in what he had said until she had climbed the stairs and got into bed, and was just drifting into a welcome slumber, when she thought vaguely, 'I wonder if he meant about the smugglers and that man . . .' and then there was a hazy, half-formed idea that he was not aware that she knew about his meeting with the smugglers. The next thing she knew, it was morning, and Annie was putting her breakfast-tray on the table by the window.

'Ah, you're awake, Miss Lucinda,' she said, coming to stand by the bed and inspect the girl's face. 'Well, you look a deal better than you did last night, I must say! It gave me a fair turn to see you so white, and coming home on that contraption—queer-looking thing, so it is! We were so worried, you know, with it getting late, and the Rector all for going out to look for you, and the Missis saying you'd probably forgotten to tell her you were visiting with Miss Martin! Well, all's well that ends well, I always says, and there's a mort of things and callers been at the door, both front and back, since first thing!'

'What things? What time is it?' Lucinda asked, sitting up gingerly and feeling the tender place on her head. As she did not turn giddy and the bump had gone down, she assumed it was safe to get out of bed, and did so.

'Why, past ten! There's your basket, come down from Pinnacles full of flowers with a real superior manservant asking how you do, and there's Mr Warrener from Cob End with a dozen rabbits and a basket of mushrooms, and Duke Howe hobbled round on his crutches with half a dozen of the neatest spools for your threads—turned them himself, he did, out of mutton-bones! That Frenchy gentleman's been with a great bunch of honey-suckles and such-like weeds, and Captain Bridges and Colonel Long with some grapes—goodness knows where they got them! And Miss Enston, of course.'

'Oh dear!' said Lucinda, sitting down to toast and jam—it was strawberry, usually kept for special occasions—and pouring herself some coffee, for the drug had made her throat feel dry and her mouth taste unpleasantly.

'*And* there's something else, left by them as we don't mention!' finished Annie with a triumphant flourish and various nods and winks and significant grimaces. 'All wrapped up in a cloth, it is.'

'Have you no work to do, Annie?' enquired Mrs Calvert frostily, sweeping into the room with a cloth-wrapped parcel in one hand and a basketful of crimson roses in the other. 'Good morning, Lucinda. Are you feeling better?'

She stooped over her daughter, offering her cheek for a filial kiss, then put down her burdens on the floor and produced a bundle of papers from her apron pocket.

'There are more gifts downstairs,' she said. 'People are very kind. Annie can bring them next time she comes upstairs. I do think red roses an inappropriate gift from a gentleman to a young lady, but they are very fine, and no doubt he meant well. The parcel was left under the ivy, where your father receives—er—other things.' She inspected the bump on Lucinda's head, pronounced it to be much better, and then sat down on the opposite side of the table and watched while Lucinda opened and read the half-dozen notes which comprised the little bundle of papers.

'How very kind of people to take the trouble!' Lucinda said, puzzling over a rather effusive offering, partly in French, from Monsieur Roland.

'You do a great deal for the folk of this town,' Mrs Calvert replied, 'and it's good to see that they appreciate it. We have much to be thankful for, that the Lord saw fit to give us such a good daughter, for I'm sure your father would have great difficulty with the parish if he did not have you to take the place which my health prevents me from filling.'

Lucinda looked at her mother with some surprise, for she had never spoken in such a vein before.

'No doubt,' Mrs Calvert continued, apparently studying something out in the garden, 'you think me a lazy creature, but I give you my word that I don't spend my time on a daybed from choice! I would much prefer to be about and doing, as becomes the wife of a clergyman, and in an emergency, I can usually rally myself to do so, but I cannot sustain it for long. A few hours of acting, contriving, organising, taking matters in hand, leaves me quite exhausted for days after. I hope, Lucinda,' turning to look most earnestly at her, 'that you may find a good husband who is all you desire within this neighbourhood, for we'd be at a loss without you. But you must not feel obliged to give up the idea of marrying a suitable gentleman, if to do so meant that you must leave Woodham. The Lord will help us, if He means you to leave us, so if your choice should fall on say, an army officer whose duties called him elsewhere, requiring you to follow, then so be it! You understand me?'

'Yes, Mama.' Lucinda went to give her mother a kiss, then sat down again. 'Thank you.'

'Well, enough of that!' Mrs Calvert said briskly. 'I am positively dying to know what is in that parcel. Pray open it.'

A paper label, saying 'Miss Calvert at the Rectory' in an untidy hand, had been pinned to the wrapping of the parcel, which was hessian roughly stitched together with twine, but Lucinda's long-suffering embroidery scissors soon had it undone. Inside, wrapped again in tissue-paper, was a length of the finest Lyons silk in a pretty sky blue, embroidered with little sprigs of flowers.

'Why, it must have cost the earth, even without the duty!' exclaimed Mrs Calvert. 'What good turn have you done to a contrabander's family, I wonder? No, I don't wonder,' she added hastily. 'It doesn't do to wonder about such folk. But such a gift! It's far too much.'

'But how can I return it, Mama?' Lucinda fingered the soft fabric with pleasure, and thought that it was ample compensation for a fright and a bumped head, for she had no doubts about why the smugglers had left it for her. She puzzled a little over how it had come so quickly, then concluded that the men she had seen had probably been on their way to meet a band coming inland from the coast, to collect goods from them and bring them back the same night. After all, if a man was away from his home for more than the duration of one night, someone would be bound to notice and perhaps tell the Preventive Officers.

'Well, of course you can't return it,' Mrs Calvert replied. 'It wouldn't do to offend them. Now, what do you mean to do with these roses?'

Lucinda spent some time, after she had washed and dressed, in arranging the roses in vases about her room. They were of a heavily scented variety and the perfume was almost overpowering, but she did not mind that, for she was too pleased to put aside her doubts and fears about Mr Harris for a while and allow herself to indulge in the foolish fancy that his gift was something more than a kindness, and the choice of red blooms had been deliberate, albeit with a melancholy undertone of knowing that it *was* only a foolish fancy, and he might turn out to be a plausible rogue after all.

The other gifts found their way up to her in stages as Annie came and went about her work. The bobbins from Duke Howe were both pretty and useful, and there were other things as well—a cucumber from Mr Morris's garden, some peaches from Mrs Willoughby, who had a glasshouse, the grapes from the two officers, and various nosegays, eggs, fruit, notes, and other things from the poorer folk of the town.

Mrs Calvert, who had left her to enjoy her gifts in peace, returned to join her for luncheon, since she was adamant that Lucinda was not to go below stairs that day. She also insisted on taking most of the roses away, for the warm weather was making the scent of them and of the honeysuckle outside the window quite unbearable.

After luncheon, Amy Martin arrived. 'Oh, my poor dear,' she exclaimed as she rushed into the room. 'I've only just heard! What on earth happened? You must tell me *everything!*'

As Mrs Calvert had left the friends alone together, Lucinda was tempted to do just that, for she had exchanged confidences with Amy for years. But she began at the beginning of the tale, and by the time she reached the point where she had walked along the Selvedge path, somehow the false version emerged, and the owl, the fall, the being found unconscious by Mr Harris, all slipped out with the glib easiness and conviction of truth.

Lucinda, who had never been used to lying, was internally horrified to find how easy it was, and troubled that she could not tell the true story even to Amy. Later, while her friend prattled about her plans for celebrating her engagement to Mr Jones, she thought miserably that she must face the fact that Mr Harris was engaged in some nefarious business, and that she must keep silence about it or she might land him in very serious trouble.

'You will be well in time, will you not?' Amy demanded suddenly.

'In time?' Lucinda asked, startled. 'I'm sorry . . . in time for what?'

'Is your head hurting you?' Amy asked solicitously. 'Am I talking too much? We're giving a dinner on

Thursday, night, to celebrate my engagement. You will be able to come, I hope?'

'Yes. I'm sorry, my mind drifted off . . . No, you're not tiring me. I'm sure I'll be able to come, for Dr Roberts said I need keep to my room only for today, and I'm much better now. Who else will be there?' She hoped her question did not sound too eager, but Amy apparently expected it, for she began to tick off on her fingers as she named the other guests.

'Your parents, of course, and the Longs, and Captain Bridges, you'll be pleased to hear! My Aunt and Uncle Jackson, and Cousin Ellie, Monsieur Roland, Mrs Willoughby, Miss Enston, of course! Dr Roberts and Mr Harris. That's eighteen, and there's not many houses in the town can sit down that many to dinner at once, I think!'

'We certainly couldn't,' Lucinda said. 'I hadn't realised that your dining-room was so large.'

'It isn't!' Amy's eyes twinkled. 'What most people don't notice is that the wall between it and Papa's study isn't a wall at all. It's a folding partition, but covered with the same dark paper as the walls, you see, so when it's closed, it don't show. Our table opens up as well, and we can put in extra leaves—if Papa can find them down in the cellar, that is, for it's an age since they were used.'

Lucinda was quite excited at the thought of so large a dinner-party until she suddenly recalled that, since her best gown was ruined by the fire, she had only her old and shabby one unless the new poplin at the dressmaker's could be finished in time. So, when Annie toiled up the stairs for the tenth time at least, to bring a tray of tea and cakes, she asked her to run to the dressmaker to enquire.

'Well, I'm sure I don't know when I'll have the time!' the maid exclaimed. 'There's Mrs Long in the garden with the Missis, and the Colonel and Mr Harris with the Rector, and Gibbs and the boy Job in the kitchen, and all wanting their teas, and Cook wanting the rabbits cut up for a pie, and me with only one pair of hands! But I'll send the boy while the tea's brewing, seeing as it's important, for you'll want that new gown for Thursday, I'll be bound.' Having delivered that speech with hardly a pause for breath, she stumped off down the stairs again, for the bell from the Rector's study could be heard in the distance.

'I wonder why the Colonel and Mr Harris are here?' mused Lucinda. 'Oh, of course—it will be about the new fire-engines, I suppose. They'll have to arrange for them to be fetched from the maker.'

"But they came yesterday. Didn't you know?' Amy exclaimed. 'I suppose it was after you went to Cob End, for it was past five when they came. The manufacturers sent them on a great wagon, with six of the biggest horses I've ever seen! It made quite a stir, for everyone in the town who wasn't still in the fields came running to see them, and there was a column of soldiers marching through the middle with fifes and drums going nineteen to the dozen, and all their wagons trundling behind, and a whole company of artillery.'

'I wonder where they were going?' Lucinda said thoughtfully. 'That's the second column to go in the past few days.'

'The fourth,' Amy corrected. 'Did you not hear them in the night? Let me see—it was Friday night; and again on Saturday night, at about midnight. The bands weren't playing, of course, but the tramp of the marching across the cobbles in the market square woke me. Do you suppose something is happening, Lucy?'

'If it is, you may be sure we'll not hear about it until it's in the newspapers! There can hardly be any men left in the camp, and yet there were twice the usual number a few days ago. Perhaps there'll be some rumours going about tomorrow.'

But there was no news from the outside world, by paper or by rumour, the next day, only local affairs occupying the tongues of the gossips. The army surgeon from the camp called at the Rectory to tell Lucinda, now quite recovered, that she had done an admirable job with Billy Warrener's arm, which should mend very well. Lucinda's new gown came home from the dress-maker and proved to be an excellent fit and very becoming. The new fire-engines were tried out during the afternoon, the smaller one hosing down the area before the church in fine style, and the larger sending a jet clear up to the roof of the pin-mill, which was four storeys high, and they were voted a great success.

The high point of the day, however, came at the end of it, when the bell-ringers assembled to ring a quarter-peal in celebration of the Curate's engagement to Miss Martin, starting at seven and going on, as Will Plomer said, until they finished, which he thought would be about ten or a little after.

Luckily, the Calverts quite enjoyed the sound of bells, for nothing else could be heard in the Rectory while they were ringing—Faith, Hope and Charity, James and John, Raphael, Michael and Gabriel, hunting up, bob-bing, dodging and hunting down, interweaving in the mathematical precision of Cambridge Surprise Major. The Rector did venture to say that he was thankful it was not a full peal, as that would last quite ten hours, but no one heard him, except possibly Fred, who seemed to be able to hear a mouse stirring even while the bells were ringing.

The Rector had sent up a barrel of ale to the ringing-chamber before they started, but a little before nine,

Lucinda went up with a trayful of bread and cheese, for at least sixteen men were taking turns to ring, and they would be glad of refreshment between turns.

There was room in the chamber for her to stand and watch for a while, after she had set out the food on the table in the corner, and she was, as always, fascinated by the concentration of the ringers, each man watching the rope of the bell next before his own, the colourful sallies flying up and down, the response of the brazen voices two stages higher in the tower, sounding strangely muffled from below, and the quiet commands of Will Plomer as he called in a relief for a man who was tiring, or set a ringer right if he was too slow or too fast.

It was a few minutes before Lucinda noticed that Mr Harris was there. He had apparently been ringing, for he was in his shirt-sleeves, over on the far side of the room, watching with absorbed interest. He glanced across at Lucinda once, and she half-lifted a hand in greeting, hoping he might come round by the wall to speak to her, but he only nodded and smiled, and presently slipped on his coat and went out.

Lucinda sighed unconsciously, and after watching another four or five rounds, she edged along the wall of the chamber to the door and went out. There was a short passage outside, and then a long, dark spiral stair, lit by an occasional tiny window, which at this time of night, framed only a starry sky. Someone had set lighted candles in each window embrasure, but the light reached only a few steps above and below, and she had to feel her way cautiously between, holding the old bell-rope looped along the outer wall, for the steps were very old and worn.

'Lucinda?' a voice whispered when she was half-way down.

'Who is it?' she breathed, but she knew the voice, even when it whispered.

'John Harris. How are you?'

'Quite recovered, thank you. Oh, and thank you for the roses, and for sending the surgeon.'

'I must speak with you quickly, before someone comes,' he cut in, almost before she had finished. He was speaking so quietly that, had he not been so close in the darkness that he was almost touching her, she might not have heard him. 'I wasn't going to say anything, but I've considered more thoroughly, and I think I'd better. Lucinda, it's important that you don't say any more about Monday night than I told your parents when I brought you home. Not to anyone!'

Lucinda made no reply, for she was trying to puzzle out whether this meant that he knew she had not been unconscious all the time.

'I mean about the fellow you saw at Pinnacles, and anything you may remember of what occurred along the Selvedge. Have you told anyone?'

'No.'

'Not a soul? Not even Miss Martin?'

'No one at all.'

'Good girl! It's vital that you keep it all to yourself. I can't tell you more at the moment, but I hope that, one day soon, I'll be able to explain it all.'

'Very well.' Lucinda was troubled by the concern in his voice, and feared for him, for he must be in great trouble to require her silence so urgently.

'Bless you!' He caught her by the shoulders and bent his head, his lips finding her cheek at first, but soon moving to her lips, hungrily demanding, and then he was gone, his feet sounding on the stairs on his way back to the ringing-chamber, leaving her shaking and breathless, pressed against the cold curve of the staircase wall.

CHAPTER TEN

THE DINNER-PARTY to celebrate the engagement of Amy Martin and Mr Jones was a great success in the estimation of everyone except Lucinda, who did not enjoy it at all. She had spent a wretched night, lying for a long time worrying about Mr Harris and his problems, alternating with fitful periods of sleep which were troubled by disturbing dreams, and so was not feeling her best from the start. To make matters worse, not fifteen minutes before the Rectory party was to set out from home, Cook brought in a jug of cream from the kitchen to ask Lucinda's opinion on whether or no it was on the turn, and in dipping in a finger to taste it, Lucinda somehow managed to drop the jug, and the cream ran in a wide stream down the front of her new gown. Being poplin, it could be washed, but not in time for the evening's entertainment, and so she had to change into her old, shabby and unbecoming yellow, with the added humiliation of arriving late at the Martins' and entering a roomful of people, who all turned to look at her.

Amy and Mrs Martin were full of commiseration when the Rector, in excusing their lateness, explained what had happened, but the Jacksons—particularly Cousin Ellie and her mother—seemed to find it amusing, tittering behind their fans and making whispered remarks to one another.

Lucinda had no great liking for the Jacksons, who

lived at Horsing and often visited the Martins, Mrs Jackson being Mrs Martin's sister, and she particularly disliked Cousin Ellie, for she combined an affectedly superior manner with a catty tongue, and, secure in her porcelain complexion, fair curls and large blue eyes, was free in her critical comments on the physical appearance and dress of anyone she encountered.

On their last meeting she had remarked that Lucinda must find her 'carroty' hair a trial, and had she considered dying it, and offered to send Amy the receipt for a bleaching lotion which might improve her 'sallow' complexion. 'Of course, being dark-haired, you cannot expect to have a naturally fair countenance, but there is no need for it to be quite so muddy, I assure you!'

'Could you not lend poor Miss Calvert something more suitable, Amy?' she drawled on this occasion. 'There is that pink gown you wore last time you came to us. I'm sure it would look quite striking on your friend!' and she and her mother fell to tittering again at the thought of auburn hair with a pink gown.

'Don't mind them, Lucy!' Amy whispered.

'I am convinced that Miss Calvert would be beautiful if she dressed in *un sac pour farine*—what you say? A flour-sack,' Monsieur Roland declared suddenly in an overloud voice, glaring at the Jackson ladies like a thundercloud.

'Hear, hear!' said Captain Bridges bravely, despite a discouraging shake of the head from the wife of his commanding officer, who thought Cousin Ellie and her like were best ignored.

'In my youth,' said Mrs Willoughby in the carrying tones and didactic manner of an English memsahib instructing the heathen, 'I frequently *prayed* that my hair might suddenly turn auburn, and my complexion that delightful creamy colour that goes with it, but, unfortunately, it persisted in remaining an uninspiring blonde! So insipid.' She gave Cousin Ellie one single glance which was more eloquent than any number of speeches.

There was an awkward pause, which Mr Harris broke, to Lucinda's great relief, by saying in a general way, 'We're fortunate with the weather this summer, apart from it turning the cream. The harvest should be excellent, I think.' Normal conversation then resumed for the few minutes remaining until dinner was served.

Naturally, Lucinda had hoped that she might sit near Mr Harris—perhaps even go in with him—but Amy, with mistaken kindness, had paired her with Monsieur Roland, and arranged that Captain Bridges should sit on her other side. Both gentlemen were attentive at any time, but this evening, no doubt feeling that she had been slighted by Cousin Ellie, they continued to rally to her support to an extent which she found embarrassing.

To make matters worse, Mr Harris had been paired with Mrs Jackson, and had Cousin Ellie on his other side; both ladies, no doubt informed by Mrs Martin of his probable income, set out to charm him, Cousin Ellie on her own account, and Mrs Jackson backing her with determination. Mr Harris wore his ironic smile and listened to their chatter with his lids drooping over those cool grey eyes and, just once, caught Lucinda's eye across the table and winked. That was the only comfort she had, for Mr Martin kept the gentlemen talking over the port for a long time, and they had hardly joined the ladies when Mrs Calvert said quietly that she had the headache and wished to go home, so, of course, the Rector and Lucinda went with her.

The next week passed in a similarly unsatisfactory manner. Lucinda had plenty to occupy her, and did actually see Mr Harris several times, but never when there was any opportunity for a private conversation. He was in church on Sunday, about the market on Tuesday, and when Lucinda went to Cob End on Wednesday she saw him two fields away and exchanged a wave of greeting. He called at Cob End for a few minutes later on, before she left, to tell her that the army surgeon had seen Billy Warrener again and was satisfied with his progress, but he went away almost immediately and was nowhere to be seen along the Selvedge as she walked home.

By Thursday night she had decided that he was avoiding her, and it took little thought to work out that his reason must be to escape any questions she might wish to ask about his mysterious dealings with the stranger to whom he had given the letter. Lucinda thought of the man as the Reformed Rogue, which seemed a suitable soubriquet.

Being a sensible girl she decided that, as she could do nothing to help him except to keep quiet about what she had seen and heard, she must wait patiently until he could explain himself, and pray that whatever trouble he might be in would be resolved before very long. Meanwhile she must keep herself busy, and not be tempted to fret or waste time in idle speculation. For all the mystery and evasion about Mr Harris, she felt an underlying confidence that he was a good man at heart, and all would be well in the end, and she had the sweet memory of that kiss on the tower stairs to sustain her.

The next day, Friday, the Rector and Mr Jones went after luncheon to see the Archdeacon, so Lucinda, having visited the sick in the morning, decided to take the opportunity to tidy the Rector's study in his absence. It was a long job, for although his books were catalogued and numbered and each had its own place on his shelves, he was in the habit of taking down a dozen or so to consult about one or two items and not putting them back, so that in the course of a few weeks the shelves became half-empty and the books were piled on chairs, on the floor or on his desk.

Once they had all been sorted and replaced, there were the papers to be seen to. He had the sensible custom of noting on each letter when he had replied to it, and writing on his notes for register entries when he had copied the information into the registers, and his Stamp Duty returns were meticulously kept, but all of them were left to accumulate on the desk-top until Lucinda had an opportunity to sort them out and put them away in the various drawers allocated to their storage.

She had almost completed her task when the front door bell rang, and as she was the nearest, Annie and Cook being in the kitchen, she went to answer it and found Captain Bridges on the doorstep.

'Good afternoon, Miss Calvert,' he said. 'Is the Rector at home? I should be glad of a few minutes' conversation with him.'

'I'm afraid not. He'll not be back until late this evening.'

The young man looked anxious, and the news that the Rector was not available obviously increased his anxiety, so she added, 'May I help at all?'

'I—I don't know,' he said uncertainly. 'I feel I must confide in someone. I don't know what to do . . .'

'Come in, then,' she said firmly, and took him into the study, where she offered him a chair, and sat down herself behind the desk in her father's place.

'It's just that I feel I must talk to someone, or burst!' the Captain said, twisting his shako round and round in his hands. 'Colonel Long told me today . . . You can keep a secret, can you not, Miss Calvert?'

'I keep many secrets,' Lucinda replied. 'People often

confide in me when my father isn't here, or if they prefer to speak to a female. I'll not betray any confidences, I promise you!'

'Thank you. Colonel Long told me today that . . . Oh, it doesn't seem possible, but he assures me it's true! He says there's a spy in the district!'

'A spy!' Lucinda exclaimed. 'You mean, someone spying for the French?'

'Yes. Of course, with the powder-mill and the camp, there are things happening here of interest to the enemy, but one can't imagine anyone one knows—with whom one is on terms of friendship . . . It's preposterous, and yet he's quite certain!'

'But how could a spy send information to France?' Lucinda asked, already half-knowing the answer.

'By means of the smugglers! In code, of course, so the carriers would think the letters to be innocent messages to a friend or a relation. Miss Calvert, it makes me sick with worry to think that I may inadvertently have told this man something which could put my fellow-countrymen's lives in danger! In conversation with someone one assumes to be as pro-British as oneself, it would be easy to let something slip, thinking no harm.'

'Who is it?' Lucinda felt that the question was too sharp and anxious, but she could not find the means to soften it.

'I don't know, and that's what makes it worse! I begged him to tell me, but he says I must wait until tomorrow, when the fellow is to be unmasked. He won't tell me before, in case I give some warning hint to him, by a word or a look . . . I accept the reasoning, but I'm so troubled to think what I may have done, and also of what must become of him . . . He must certainly be someone known to me, someone I know well—thought I knew well, that is—and it's such a dreadful death!'

'Death?' Lucinda was startled.

'Hanging.' The Captain looked quite sickened at the word. 'They hang spies. I know one is no more dead after it than by being killed by a bullet or a cannon-ball, but it's the time before—knowing, and the loneliness . . . I'd not wish that on any man, whatever he's done.'

'No.' Lucinda spoke in a small, remote voice, her thoughts all with the man she loved, who was in such terrible danger. She closed her eyes for a moment and made herself shut those thoughts away, for she must first help Captain Bridges to deal with his doubts and self-torments.

'I don't think it likely that you would have let anything of importance slip out,' she said. 'You're always very discreet about whatever happens at the camp, and, if you recall, when Colonel Congreve started talking about his rockets at dinner that time, it was you who turned the conversation in order to stop him. As for the man, we must pray for him. It's all we can do to help him, and he needs our help, even if he is our enemy.'

'Yes.' Captain Bridges gave a deep sigh. 'Thank you, Miss Calvert. You're very understanding. I feel much better for having talked to you, and I shall pray for him. But I wish I knew who it was. There are two or three men in this town whom I regard very highly, and it would be dreadful if it should prove to be one of them.'

'You've no idea?' Lucinda was still fighting against a growing certainty.

'None at all. Well, I'll not keep you any longer. Many thanks again, Miss Calvert. You've been a great help.' He stood up to depart.

Lucinda saw him out, then returned to the study, where she finished sorting the papers, but not giving them her full attention, so that her father was later surprised to find the account for Communion wine included in the inventory of church valuables, and wondered if his daughter was tactfully suggesting that he was paying too much for it. After that, she sat thinking and praying until dinner-time, when the Rector returned with much to say about the iniquities of the Archdeacon and various other clerical matters, and so did not notice how quiet and abstracted Lucinda was.

In the early hours of the morning she finally reached a decision about the relative importance of her patriotic duty and her responsibility towards the man she loved. After all, the important thing was to prevent him from doing further harm to her country, and that could be effected without his being arrested and sent to trial, if he could be warned in time. Consequently, she was up and dressed by the time Mr Gibbs started to ring the apprentice bell, and slipped down the stairs and out of the house under cover of its sound.

Normally she would have enjoyed crossing the fields so early in the morning, with the shadow of the trees lying long across the dew-wet grass, and the air still chill and fresh, but she had no thought this morning for anything except reaching Pinnacles. She passed patches of blue scabious and corn-cockle, fields of ripe corn studded with scarlet poppies and a whole flock of sheep without seeing any of them, and even walked through the middle of Mr Harris's herd of cows without a second thought.

It seemed an age before she reached the steps up from the Selvedge path to the lowest terrace of his garden, and toiled up one flight after another, her muslin frock wet almost to the knees with dew, brushing past rosebushes heavy with flowers which shed their fragrant petals to cling to the damp cloth. The long windows of the small parlour in which she had seen the Reformed Rogue stood open to the morning, and she walked in through them without hesitation.

Mr Harris was sitting at the table, eating a boiled egg in a silver egg-cup. The table was covered by a snowy cloth, and set with a rack of toast, a dish of butter and another of honey, and a fragrantly steaming pot of coffee. The cat Charlotte was sitting upright on a chair opposite Mr Harris, regarding him steadily over the edge of the table, and he was saying to her, 'No, you may not eat my egg! You'll have your breakfast in the kitchen, madam!' when Lucinda entered.

'You'll have to go quickly,' she said baldly. 'They're coming to arrest you today!'

Mr Harris stood up, dropping his egg-spoon and napkin on the table, looked a little surprised, and said mildly, 'Good morning, my dear! May I offer you some coffee?'

'There isn't time!' she said desperately. 'Don't you understand? They'll hang you if you don't escape!' She was afflicted by a terrible sense of unreality, and wondered if she was dreaming.

'If I'm to flee the country, I'll not go on an empty stomach!' he replied with unruffled calm, and rang the bell. George answered with alacrity and fetched another cup, some fresh toast and more coffee without betraying the slightest trace of surprise at finding a visitor for breakfast.

'Now,' said Mr Harris when Lucinda was sitting at the table with a cup of coffee before her, 'I'll warrant you've rushed up here without waiting to eat or drink anything, so help yourself to toast, and tell me why I'm to be hanged, for I find it a novel idea!'

'Captain Bridges told me yesterday that Colonel Long had warned him there's a spy in the district, and that he's to be arrested today,' she said. 'Captain Bridges doesn't know yet who it is, but . . .'

'But you think you do?' Mr Harris buttered another piece of toast and absent-mindedly offered it to Charlotte, who jumped down from her chair, seized the offering, and settled down on a priceless oriental silk rug to lick the butter off it. Mr Harris looked at his empty plate in a puzzled fashion, and took another piece of toast for himself.

'I wasn't unconscious for long, you see,' Lucinda said, and then stopped, wondering why he was so calm, for she had been too engrossed in her need to convince him of his danger to notice the incident of the misdirected toast.

'Well, I knew that, of course!' He added honey to the butter. 'There's a deal of difference in the feel of an unconscious body, and that of a conscious one. It suited me, however, to avoid the need for explanations, and it saved the smugglers worrying about whether you recognised them and what you might be inclined to do about it.' Apparently thinking he had given her a reasonable explanation, he took a bite of toast and looked at her expectantly.

'I heard you mention letters to the smugglers,' she went on. 'You gave them one, and received one from them, which you passed to the—to that man who was here. Then there were Colonel Long's papers, which were in his pocket when he gave you his coat on the night of the fire, but were missing when he had his coat again. They were under the peony in the garden just after you called the next morning, although they certainly had not been there an hour before. I've seen you with your telescope, watching the army camp, and you know more than anyone outside the powder-mill about Colonel Congreve's rockets . . .'

Mr Harris took another piece of toast and buttered it. 'A damning collection of evidence!' he said agreeably.

'Then, of course, I begged you to keep silence about my—er—nefarious activities.'

'And you speak French,' Lucinda added wretchedly, wondering why he seemed so unaffected by her revelations. 'And you have a book in French about codes and cyphers, and all those sheets of paper with letters set out on them . . . There's a simple code, I believe, where you spell out your message on, say, every sixth letter, and fill in the rest with nonsense, or with an ordinary sort of letter . . .' She thought that statement sounded confusing, with the two meanings of the word 'letter'.

'Is there, by George!' said Mr Harris in an interested tone.

'I read about it in a book.' Lucinda took a gulp of coffee, then, suddenly feeling hungry, took a piece of toast and buttered it. 'I don't know why you should wish to betray England to our enemies, for I don't think you're an evil man, and I wouldn't want you to be . . . to be hanged, so will you please run away, before they come?'

'Lucinda,' Mr Harris said softly and earnestly, 'you're an intelligent and brave girl. You've put your evidence together very well, reasoned it out quite thoroughly, and risked a great deal to come here and warn me! Did it not occur to you that I might take you for a hostage, or even kill you in order to make my escape more easily?'

'I didn't think for one moment that you'd harm me. Oh, please! I'm not joking! How can you sit calmly eating toast, when they may be here any moment to arrest you?'

'Because, my dear girl, they're not coming until this evening,' he said quietly. 'The arresting party is to dine with me, and I expect the unmasking will take place then, if all goes to plan.'

'But you must still go now,' she cried passionately, 'so

that you may be further from their reach! Oh how can you sit there, eating toast, when you may be hanged?'

Mr Harris regarded her for a moment, but without his usual touch of irony, and his eyes were not in the least cool but so warm that Lucinda, her heart thumping uncomfortably, hastily ate her piece of toast and reached for another.

'There is something very comforting about toast when one's emotions are in anything of a turmoil,' he remarked absently. 'Look, m'dear—I don't think it will come to a hanging—at least, I hope not, but I have to be present at my dinner-party for reasons which I cannot explain at present. Would it embarrass you to be the only lady present at such a gathering? I should like you to be there, to hear the answers to all your questions. Will you come?'

Lucinda hesitated, filled with despair. How could she bear to see him unmasked as a villain and arrested, but how much harder to sit at home, wondering and fearing . . . 'I should like to,' she said. 'But I don't know if my parents would allow it.'

'Your father will be coming himself, and I'll send him a note during the day to ask him to bring you with him. I'm sure I can persuade him. Will you come?'

'Yes,' she replied miserably, and groped in her reticule for a handkerchief, with which she blew her nose in a manner which her mother would not have approved.

He smiled and poured her some more coffee, then said in an ordinary conversational tone, 'The cottages will be finished by the end of next week, and my sheep will be here the week after, and I fully intend to survive to see my plans carried out, so try not to worry! Very well, Charlotte'—for the cat was patting his leg and mewing—'I've not forgotten your milk,' and he poured her a dishful, which she received as of right and lapped industriously.

Lucinda, feeling at the same time despondent, puzzled and, somehow, very slightly hopeful, ate more toast, then recollected that she did not wish her parents to be alarmed at her unexplained absence, and so must go home at once. Mr Harris walked with her to the bottom of the hill, talking easily about cows and sheep and donkeys, of which he was very fond, and other impersonal matters.

Then, when they reached the stile at the edge of his land, he took Lucinda's hand in both of his, and said, 'Don't imagine that I undervalue what you tried to do for me today. I can guess what agonies of mind and conscience it must have cost you, and I am deeply grateful. I wish I might tell you that all will be well, but I fear you will find the truth painful, and the waiting to hear it distressing. I'm sorry. I can only assure you that, if all goes as I plan, there will be no loss of life, by hanging or any other method. Try to trust me, and I hope to see you this evening.' He kissed her hand, and then her cheek.

She gave a little sob, clinging to his hand, and he drew her close, put his arms round her and held her comfortingly for a few moments. 'I'm so sorry,' he whispered. 'I'd give anything for matters to be otherwise so you might be spared distress, but I cannot help it.'

She drew away from him, looked at his face uncertainly, then stumbled away homeward, stopping once or twice to shed a few tears and praying incoherently all the way that things should turn out as well as possible for him, even if it meant a long imprisonment.

'If he must go to prison,' she decided, 'I shall visit him and take him whatever he needs. I shall do what I can, and surely Father will help me, for it says in the Bible that we must visit prisoners . . .'

She passed a wretched day, trying to keep busy and appear as usual, fearful that any sign of distress might be taken for illness and prevent her going to Pinnacles in the evening. Her lateness for breakfast was unquestioned, for her father simply said, 'A lovely morning for an early walk, although I fear that we may have rain later. Did I tell you, my dear, that I shall be out for dinner? A little matter of business.'

The note from Mr Harris arrived as they were sitting down to luncheon, and Mr Calvert, looking surprised, said, 'Lucinda, my dear, Mr Harris particularly asks that I bring you with me this evening. Would this be convenient?'

'Why, yes, Father. I'm not otherwise engaged.'

She glanced uneasily at her mother, who murmured something about gentlemen not being able to get their numbers right for dinner, apparently under the impression that Mr Harris had suddenly found himself with thirteen to sit down, or some similar calamity. 'I shall retire early with a tray, as I find this continuing warm weather very trying. I hope it may not thunder!' she concluded.

At one time during the afternoon a mass of dark clouds came up, but they passed over without actually doing anything, and the sun was shining again by the time the Rectory carriage set out for Pinnacles, with Lucinda, full of nervous anticipation, dressed in the new poplin gown, the cream stain carefully washed out, sitting opposite her father, wondering what she was to hear during the evening.

As the carriage mounted the hill, the Rector said seriously, 'I have an inkling of the purport of this gathering, my dear, for I had a letter from London a short time ago, telling me certain things which I thought it best to keep to myself, and also I've had a long discussion with some of my friends concerning the same matter. I believe that tonight we shall be hearing more about it, but I can say nothing now, except to warn you to be prepared for a shock.'

To which Lucinda could only reply, 'Yes, Father.'

The gathering was quite small, and Lucinda was not surprised to find Colonel Long and Captain Bridges there, and it seemed reasonable that Mr Martin and Monsieur Roland should also have been invited, for Mr Martin was a solicitor and a magistrate, which would be useful if anyone was to be arrested. The Frenchman could act as an interpreter if necessary, and his deep hatred for the present régime in his country would make him an interested party in the thwarting of a French spy.

The gentlemen were surprised at Lucinda's arrival, but Mr Harris said airily, 'I've asked Miss Calvert for a special reason, for we cannot celebrate the establishment of my farming venture without her, since she has been instrumental in finding me some of the essential parts of it. Shall we go in, as we're all here?'

The dinner was informal, and no doubt the food was delicious and the wine of the first quality, but Lucinda was so keyed up, waiting for what was to come, that she ate and drank without tasting or noticing what was set before her.

At last the dishes were removed, coffee brought in, and the servants withdrew. Mr Harris, with a distinct change from easy affability to a steely, businesslike tone, said, 'Now, Miss Calvert, gentlemen! To the matter we are met to discuss. It appears, Monsieur Roland, that you are not all that you would have us believe.'

This gentleman, who had been sitting back, contemplating his coffee-cup in the pleasant aftermath of a good dinner, gave a start of surprise and said, 'I, m'sieur? What do you mean?'

'There are a number of small matters concerning you which require explanation,' Mr Harris replied grimly. 'For example, the letters which you pay the smugglers so handsomely to carry to France for you!'

'My letters?' He looked bewildered. 'I cannot imagine 'ow you come to know of them. Yes, I send letters to France, and receive them, too. My sister is still living in Calais, and we keep in touch, for we are the only two left of our family!'

'Yes. Charming letters, full of idle gossip and brotherly concern!' Mr Harris still sounded grim. 'Sometimes the spelling is a little odd, or a construction not quite as the *Académie* would have it, but it's not easy to write correctly when one is incorporating a code message, is it?'

'Code? I? No, you are mistaken!' Monsieur Roland sounded amazed and indignant. 'What right 'ave you to intercept my correspondence and read it?'

'The third letter, then the seventh, then the fourth, in a regular sequence,' Mr Harris said by way of a reply. 'You shouldn't have taken the smugglers for fools, you know! The first letter you bribed them to carry was taken straight to Colonel Long, who sent it to the Horse Guards. It took a colleague of mine a week or so to discover your code, but after that it was simple to read your messages and substitute a forged one of our own from time to time. In fact, you've been very useful to us, especially in these last few weeks!'

The Frenchman's face had turned a sickly colour, but he still managed to speak quite calmly. 'Is this a joke of some sort?' he enquired.

'No more of a joke than those sums of money paid into your account at Rothschild's bank in London,' Mr Harris replied. 'An interesting family, the Rothschilds, you know—there's an uncle here, a cousin there, a brother somewhere else—all bankers, spread about the chief cities of Europe. Wars and frontiers are no more than a mild inconvenience to them, for they have their own system of transfers and their own courier service. The payments into your London account come by way of two neutral countries, but they originate in Paris! Nothing to say, m'sieur? I'll tell you some more curious facts, then.

'You noticed the activity about the powder-mill and the camp a while ago, the sudden movement of barges along the Navigation, and of soldiers marching off towards the coast, for you reported it all in your letters—and very accurately too! You formed the wrong conclusion, however, for it was not the beginnings of another expedition to the Netherlands, as you thought. In fact, if the wind has held steady, I imagine that our ships are using those rockets which interested you so much to bombard Copenhagen! Colonel Congreve may even be there with them, for a force of the Royal Hanoverian Army, in which he serves, is advancing through Denmark, and even your old acquaintance Sir Arthur Wellesley is there with a landing force!'

'Copenhagen!' exclaimed Monsieur Roland before anyone else could speak.

'Yes.' Mr Harris smiled in a sardonic fashion. 'The papers you filched from Colonel Long's pocket said Holland again, did they not? It was intended that the Colonel should contrive to drop them where you would find them, but you saved him the trouble by searching his pockets while you were so kindly hanging his coat on the back of a chair.'

'But Denmark's neutral!' Captain Bridges sounded shocked.

'In the recently signed treaty between Bonaparte and Alexander of Russia,' Mr Harris explained, 'there are several secret clauses, according to a friend of ours who pursues a similar calling to m'sieur, but does so in Russia. One of those clauses is an agreement that Bonaparte should invade Denmark in order to seize the Danish fleet, to replace the ships he lost at Trafalgar. Unfortunately for him, and thanks to our friend, by the time his men reach Copenhagen the ships will be ours or they'll be useless wrecks, depending how long it takes the Danes to accept reality. I'm afraid there are no neutrals in Europe any more—everyone must either fight Bonaparte or surrender to him! We let your report on the proposed invasion of Holland go through, for it saved the trouble of forging something of a similarly misleading nature. That odd little man you saw here, Miss Calvert, was a forger, you see. It was convenient for him to be close at hand when the smugglers brought an outgoing letter, in case it needed—er—altering. If he forged a substitute, he could also carry the original back to our masters in the Horse Guards.'

'How do you come to be involved in this?' Captain Bridges asked, giving the impression that he thought it an odd interest for a gentleman, and not one of which he approved.

'I have a natural flair for breaking codes, and I've made a study of them,' Mr Harris replied. 'Also I speak, read and write French well enough to decode Monsieur Roland's letters, and write a substitute, when necessary, for the forger to copy. I used to come secretly to Colonel Long's house to do it, but I discovered that this estate, which is exactly what I have been seeking for some time, was conveniently close at hand, so I've been continuing the operation from here since I moved in. Well, m'sieur, have you nothing to say to all this?'

The Frenchman gave a very gallic shrug, and replied, 'What is there left for me to say? There is much I would wish to add, but 'oo would believe me?'

'Why don't you try us?' Mr Harris sounded quite kind and gentle. 'Don't mistake our feelings towards you, m'sieur! You're a brave man, and worthy of respect, for you've chosen to serve your country in a dangerous, difficult and very lonely manner. Say what is in your mind.'

He gave another, subtly different, shrug, and said, 'Then I will tell you that I am deeply grateful for the kindness and friendship I 'ave received in this place. I regret that, in the nature of my task, I was trying to bring 'arm on you all, but it was not out of 'atred of you or your country, only out of love for my own! If I could 'ave my dearest wish, France and England would live at peace, and I would choose, I think, to make my 'ome 'ere. Does that sound strange from an enemy spy? I accept that I am finished, so do as you will with me!'

There was a moment or two of silence, and then Captain Bridges cleared his throat nervously and said, 'I say . . . do we—er—have to arrest him? I mean, would it be . . . After all, as long as he stops spying . . .'

'Could he not go back to France with the smugglers?' Lucinda added. 'If he's in France, he can't be doing any spying here, can he?' She had sat through the revelations concerning Monsieur Roland in a trance of relief, shock, joy and amazement, and only now came to her senses, being quite surprised to find herself capable of speaking at all.

'I have no warrant for anyone's arrest,' Mr Harris replied with a very blank face. 'I've not even told the Horse Guards that I'm putting an end to Monsieur Roland's activities, for that's within my discretion. I've no doubt there are stirrings up there as it begins to penetrate those brass helmets that the man has outlived his usefulness now, and it's time to be rid of him. Too bad if he disappears before they translate thought into action! If I were you, Monsieur Roland, I'd go off tonight with the contrabanders.'

'Are you serious?' The Frenchman was suddenly alert.

'Perfectly. You'll find them waiting for you in the usual place,' Mr Harris replied briskly. 'They've collected your books and essentials from your lodging, and your passage is already paid. You'll need some of the ready, so I've taken the liberty of withdrawing this from your account at Rothschild's!' He tossed him a clinking bag, which was caught deftly. 'You'd best be off before they grow tired of waiting.' He stood up and held out his hand to the Frenchman, who shook it in a diffident manner. 'Good luck to you!'

The others rose and shook hands with him with varying degrees of reluctance, Mr Martin hardly being able to bring himself to extend his hand at all. Lucinda gave hers freely, for she had always liked Monsieur Roland, and could, to some extent, understand his feelings. He raised it to his lips, and said softly, 'I owe so much more than I can tell to you, Miss Calvert. I shall never forget you! I bid you all adieu! Thank you all.' And he slipped out through the open windows into the night.

'Well, that's that, then!' said Mr Harris as they resumed their seats. 'Now, are there any questions left unanswered?'

'Why did you let him go?' Mr Martin sounded angry.

'Would you rather see him hang?' Mr Harris asked crisply. 'You've obviously thought well enough of him to have him to dine at your table. Is a man to be despised for serving his country in the best way he knows? Is he any less brave than the soldier who sets out to kill his enemy with a musket? Should we think any less of

Monsieur Roland than of our own spy who sent us news
of the secret clauses of the Treaty of Tilsit? In any case,
"our sorrows come, not single spies, but in battalions",
so surely we may let the single spy go, for he'll do us no
more harm!'

Mr Martin was silent, and only shook his head doubtfully. Mr Calvert, after waiting a moment to see if he
meant to argue the point, said, 'May I enquire, Mr
Harris—who are you?'

'My name really is John Harris,' he replied, smiling.
'But I'm more usually known as Viscount Cressing.
M'father's the Earl of Gorseley, who's usually away
being an ambassador or plenipotentiary somewhere or
other.'

Lucinda felt that he had just dealt her the worst shock
of the whole evening, and she was surprised to hear
herself say, in her normal voice, 'Why was he so sure that
he saw you in Paris in '02? What was the point of lying
about it?'

'Neither of us was lying,' Mr Harris replied, looking
directly at her. 'He must have seen my brother Edward.
We're much alike, and he was certainly in Paris during
the Peace of Amiens, on the staff of Lord Cornwallis,
our ambassador, so he'd have had good reason to call on
the French Foreign Minister.'

The party broke up soon after, for everyone present
had liked the Frenchman, and, apart from the two who
had known his real nature, they were all shocked by the
evening's revelations.

Mr Harris placed Lucinda's shawl about her shoulders
with some solicitude while the gentlemen were assuming
their coats and hats in the entrance-hall, and took the
opportunity to whisper, 'I'm sorry, my dear! You
must have spent a most wretched day, and such sad
news at the end of it. I wish I could have told you

the truth this morning, but there were so many other considerations . . . Can you forgive me?'

'I'm so glad it wasn't you, that nothing else matters,' she replied tremulously, 'and poor Monsieur Roland will be safe, will he not? I think he really wanted to go home, so perhaps it's all for the best.' She did not look up at his face, being occupied with smoothing her gloves as she spoke, which was unfortunate, as she might have learned something from his expression.

He pressed the hand she offered him in farewell, and said, 'You have a good heart, my dear. Any man should be grateful to count you his friend!'

Lucinda and her father were silent most of the way home, lost in their own thoughts, but as the carriage rattled along East Street, Mr Calvert said, 'I'm glad you spoke as you did, Lucinda. I'd not wish you or me to be concerned in sending a man to the gallows without trying to save him!'

'No, Father,' Lucinda replied in a subdued voice. She felt quite numb with shock, partly from the discovery that a man she had liked, even admired, and sympathised with in his loneliness and home-sickness, should have lived such a lie in all the years she had known him, and partly from the realisation that Mr Harris, whom she loved and who had seemed at least interested in her, who had spoken to her in, she felt sure, affectionate terms, and of whom she had dared to daydream with a growing belief that her dreams might come true, should have become, in the course of one sentence, utterly unattainable.

'I suppose,' she thought wretchedly, when at last the explanations to her mother were over and she had escaped to her own room, 'I suppose that gentlemen in the highest ranks of Society think nothing of stealing a kiss from a female so much lower in rank, and calling her by her Christian name! It wouldn't occur to him that I might build hopes on something so trivial . . .' She shed more than a few tears over her loss of a friend, and the more grievous loss of one she had begun to hope might be a husband.

Mrs Calvert felt well enough to attend church in the morning, despite the expected break in the weather, which brought a grey sky and a fine mizzle of rain that accorded well with Lucinda's feelings.

The erstwhile Mr Harris was in the Pinnacles pew, looking no different as a Viscount than he had as a plain Mister, and Lucinda was pleased to see that, immediately after the service, Mr Martin stepped across the aisle to speak to him and shake him by the hand. She had no opportunity to speak to him herself, for Mr Gibbs had heard rumours of the previous night's doings and was lurking in the vestry with intent to extract as much information as possible from Lucinda. She found most of his questions difficult to answer, and by the time she escaped from him, Lord Cressing had gone.

The afternoon seemed long and tedious. A Sabbath peace descended on the Rectory after luncheon, with Mrs Calvert dozing in the parlour while Lucinda tried to concentrate on a book of very dull sermons which her father had recommended as suitable Sunday reading. Mr Calvert was in his study, contemplating his sermon for Evensong with his eyes closed, and the servants were, no doubt, taking a nap in the kitchen. Fred was awake, for Lucinda could see him from the parlour window, draped on a branch of the walnut tree, watching the swifts flying about the church eaves.

Suddenly the front door bell jangled, and Lucinda went quickly to answer it before it woke everyone. To her surprise, Lord Cressing was standing on the step, sheltering under an umbrella.

'Good afternoon,' he said. 'Is the Rector at home? I wonder if I might have a few words with him?'

With a strong feeling of *déjà vu*, Lucinda invited him to enter, lodged his wet umbrella in a particularly ugly vase which lived behind the front door, and took him to the study, much preoccupied with wondering whether she should have curtsied when she saw him. The Rector rose to greet him with, 'Why, Mr—that is, my lord! This is a pleasant surprise! You see, I have no difficulty in identifying you with my excellent new spectacles. I shall not accuse you this time of coming to put up the banns!'

'As a matter of fact,' Lord Cressing said with surprising diffidence, 'I hope I may actually request you to enter my name in your banns register before I leave. I'm come to ask your permission to speak to Miss Calvert!'

'Speak to Lucinda?' The Rector looked at his daughter in a puzzled fashion, then light dawned. 'Oh, you mean *speak* to her! Oh, my goodness! Well, yes—by all means! I—er—you'd best—er—speak in here! I'll go to—er . . .' He stammered himself over to the door, and paused in the opening. 'I'll leave it a trifle ajar, for Mrs Grundy's benefit, you understand . . .' and went out.

Lucinda, standing transfixed by her father's desk, heard him go to the parlour, and the rumble of his voice as he spoke to his wife in a loud whisper. Then Mrs Calvert uttered, 'A Viscount!' in what might, in a less genteel person, have been described as a small shriek. 'Pray, Mr Calvert, pass me my smelling-bottle!' Then the parlour door closed.

Lord Cressing cleared his throat nervously, muttered something which sounded like 'Nothing ventured,' and took a step nearer to Lucinda, who had clasped her hands together to stop them trembling, and was staring fixedly at a worn patch on the carpet, wondering when she would wake up. He secured her clasped hands between his own, took a deep breath, opened his lips to speak, and then received an unexpected interruption, for a portly form insinuated itself through the small gap which the Rector had left between the door and jamb, and enquired loudly what the gentleman was about.

It was, of course, not Mrs Grundy, but Fred who advanced upon his friend with great interest.

Lord Cressing retained his hold upon Lucinda's hands, and said to the cat, 'You're quite right! I've made a regular pig's nest of the whole business, have I not? No wonder she greets me without a smile, or even a look! What am I to do, Fred? Will you speak to her for me?'

Fred sat down, arranging his tail neatly about his stubby paws, and regarded the two humans with a noncommittal stare.

'Be a good fellow, now!' Lord Cressing said coaxingly. 'Tell her I love her more than anything in the world, and it broke my heart to hurt her yesterday. Did Monsieur Roland mean so much to her, d'you think, that she can't forgive me for destroying her belief in him and driving him away?'

'Of course not!' Lucinda replied breathlessly on Fred's behalf. The man's hands were warm and felt real enough, but surely this could not really be happening? She could not have heard him say what he had just said . . . could she?

'Never?' Lord Cressing's voice cracked on the word.

There was a moment's confused silence, and then Lucinda, realising that he had misunderstood her, hastily said, 'No! I mean yes! Oh, what I'm trying to say is . . . I *did* like Monsieur Roland, and I was sorry for him, and I'm glad you let him escape, but I'm much more glad that it wasn't you! I did say so last night, did I not?' with a sudden doubt.

'So I thought, but you avoided me this morning, and

seemed not at all pleased to see me this afternoon . . . Oh, my dear girl! Is it really all right?'

Thinking he meant the matter of forgiving him for revealing the truth about Monsieur Roland, Lucinda replied, 'Yes, of course!' and was startled when he gave a great sigh, dropped on one knee and held on to her hands even more tightly.

'Oh, you mustn't!' she exclaimed in confusion. Fred, apparently feeling *de trop*, made a stately exit.

'But I must!' Lord Cressing replied firmly. 'I'll not defer knowing my fate another moment! Will you marry me, Lucinda?'

'How can I?' she replied wretchedly. 'A Viscount doesn't marry the daughter of a country parson.'

'I'm only a courtesy Viscount!'

'But you'll be an Earl one day, and that's even worse.'

'It has nothing to do with it. Look, Lucinda, if it was plain John Harris saying to Lucinda Calvert, "I love you. Will you marry me?" what would you say?'

Lucinda looked at him, saw the expression in his eyes, knew that she could never have dreamed such a look, and answered, 'I would say, "I love you. Yes, I'll marry you."'

John Harris, plain or otherwise, grinned with relief, and in one swift movement rose to his feet and took her in his arms. Lucinda said inconsequentially, 'Fred will be pleased!' and then he bent his head to kiss her. She had never dreamed that a kiss could be anything like that, and it seemed to get better every moment, so that, when the bells suddenly began to ring for Evensong, she realised that they were anything but a manifestation of her own ecstasy only when the courtesy Viscount murmured, '"How soft the music of those village bells!"' between kisses.

Six exciting series for you every month... from Harlequin

Harlequin Romance·
The series that started it all

Tender, captivating and heartwarming...
love stories that sweep you off to faraway places
and delight you with the magic of love.

◆

Harlequin Presents·
Powerful contemporary love stories...as individual as the women who read them

The No. 1 romance series...
exciting love stories for you, the woman of today...
a rare blend of passion and dramatic realism.

◆

Harlequin Superromance®
It's more than romance...
it's Harlequin Superromance

A sophisticated, contemporary romance-fiction
series, providing you with a longer,
more involving read...a richer mix of complex plots,
realism and adventure.